Dedication

To Marion and Delbert

Sunrise Interrupted

The Martel Sisters – Book Three

Eden Monroe

Print ISBNs
Amazon print 9780228629825
Ingram Spark 9780228629832
Barnes & Noble 9780228629856
BWL Print 9780228629849

Copyright 2022 by Linda Hersey
Cover art by Pandora Designs

Table of Contents

Prologue

The old dog, soaked from a tumble into the icy water and limping badly, continued to pick its way along the creek that rushed between steep boulder-strewn banks. Beau Remington, far above on horseback, spotted the bedraggled canine and quickly dismounted, clamouring down the embankment toward it. With one arm wrapped around a sturdy yellow birch to anchor himself, he stretched forward to scoop up the small dog and slipped it inside his jacket. Steadying the terrified animal with one hand he then began the climb back up to the trail where his horse, Chance, waited patiently.

He talked to the dog soothingly, the rich timbre of his voice comforting as the shivering slowly began to subside within the warmth of leather on a cool spring day. Beau urged the gelding into a trot for the final half-mile to his ranch nestled deep in the rolling hills of Belleisle, New Brunswick, Canada's picture province. He loved the quiet solitude, but soon the area would have some unlikely visitors when they started shooting the movie, Retribution, a few miles up the road. As a veterinarian he'd already agreed to be on set when animals were scheduled to appear in the movie, so it should be an interesting experience.

The dog whimpered plaintively against him, reigniting Beau's anger at the insensibility of some selfish, cold-hearted pet owners. This had definitely been a dump, an old dog, half-blind and likely no longer wanted. The poor thing had either been lame before being abandoned, or injured in the fall, and it was because of situations like this that he'd dedicated his life to animals.

* * *

Alexandra Martel studied her reflection in the mirror, leaning in for a closer look. She'd consistently received good reviews for her acting ability, but in show business it was also appearance. Everyone knew that. At thirty-one she was hardly over the hill, but the camera came at you with uncompromising scrutiny. That reminded her, she had an appointment at her favourite spa today for an anti-aging facial. She was fortunate to have been blessed with a flawless complexion, but it still had to be maintained as time continued its relentless march forward. Workouts at the gym and a healthy lifestyle were also part of her daily regimen.

She had carved out a decent career for herself in Canada but was recently cast in the coveted role of Sari Patton in Retribution, a US feature film set for production in her home province of New Brunswick. It would be a challenging role, not only because of its demanding physicality, but also considering the director's reputation for being nearly impossible to please. Even so, Nigel Garretson had a long string of directorial successes. Her leading man was James Langford, an award-winning American actor who, after Retribution, was off to star in Twice Dead of the Sullivan At Large franchise based on the bestselling novels of the same name. A deadly handsome bad boy whose reputation preceded him, she'd been warned she'd have her hands full with him.

She sighed. She'd come a long way from high school musicals, but the big prize south of the border remained as elusive as ever, even after twelve long years in the business. Her agent, in whom she placed her utmost confidence, had been unable so far to make any significant inroads in Tinsel Town, save for a two-liner in an American soap opera and a brief appearance on a failing sitcom. Retribution could be her breakout role, the perfect opportunity to prove she was more than just another pretty face. She was also looking forward to being back in New Brunswick.

* * *

And the man watched the beautiful actress with the incredible blue eyes. Frustration ate at him like battery acid as he waited for the right moment to get close to her. He imagined easy access once she was in New Brunswick, and he'd be ready. One little slip up, and he'd have her.

Chapter 1

Alexandra switched off the jets and reached for the towel looped over the shower pole. It had been a tough day on set, and she'd needed that nice long hot shower to help her unwind, loosen knotted muscles. She flexed her shoulders before wrapping the mauve towel around her hair, then stepped out onto the fluffy mat and grabbed a matching bath sheet. She heard something. It sounded like singing. Yes, it was definitely a man singing, and off-tune at that. There was someone in the trailer with her!

Flipping the lock on the bathroom door she quickly dried off and hauled on her clothes that a few minutes ago were destined for laundry pick-up. She felt somewhat braver when she'd finished dressing, in fact she was now good and angry as she unlocked the door and stepped out into the hall to see what was going on. She remembered just as quickly these trailers were in very close proximity to each other at the movie location's basecamp, so it could be someone next door.

Glancing toward the living room she did a double take when she saw a pair of men's legs crossed at the knee, the doorframe blocking her view as to who was making themselves at home in her easy chair. The singing had stopped, mercifully, but she knew without taking another step who her visitor was, and she didn't have to wait long to confirm it. James Langford!

"Finally! Hello, baby," he announced when she strode into the living room and stopped, hands on hips. He smiled. "I thought you were never going to finish with that shower. The water table must have dropped a foot by now even if there is a river nearby."

"What are you doing in here, James? I know the door was locked, I made sure of it before I went into the bathroom."

He laughed heartily as though that was the funniest thing he'd heard all day, before taking another sip from a glass of ginger coloured liquor. "I never met a lock I couldn't pick. It's one of my many talents as you'll see when you drop that good little girl act. You're playing my wife, remember?" he asked unnecessarily. "Sari Patton isn't such a nice girl, and it'd be good for your performance to stay in character. I know you're a method actor. Soooo naughty on set, naughty off set if you get my drift."

"What makes you think my performance needs any help, naughty or otherwise?" she challenged him, happy to do so because she guessed so few women did.

He shrugged, attempting nonchalance although his gaze was keen. "You could have been a little more into that cuddling scene today. You were stiff as a board. Everyone saw it."

She'd hoped it hadn't been as noticeable as it felt, although Nigel, the director *had* called her aside and suggested she loosen up a bit. Usually he gave it to an actor right between the eyes in front of everyone, but for some reason he'd been in a more charitable frame of mind today. And she had tried to relax but the truth of it was, even in her brief career in front of the camera, no one had turned her off as badly as James Langford. He was way too friendly onscreen. *He* certainly got into the cuddling without any directorial encouragement. She instinctively didn't like the man but acknowledged that he heavily outranked her. He had more than one coveted trophy on his mantle. He was the big name for this picture whereas she was still a nobody in terms of star power.

"I didn't think today was *that* bad," she lied, lifting her chin for emphasis and never in the mood to be intimidated by him or anyone else. Well the director, but that was different. "I see my character as a bit standoffish, not a pushbutton sex machine."

He snorted. "Standoffish! Hardly! She is madly in love with her husband no matter how he treats her. I think we have the same script, or did you get the wrong copy?"

He was right. She tamped down a sarcastic reply, still angry with him for jimmying her lock. Coming into her trailer like he did was way over the line and for that blatant behavior alone she would do battle with him.

"James, get out of my trailer, now! You have no right to be in here. I was taking a shower, I could have come out of the bathroom naked for heaven's sake."

He chuckled, amused by her indignation. "What would that matter? You're my onscreen wife. We'll be seeing each other naked before we're done here anyway, next week if we keep on schedule."

She was reminded of the dreaded nude scene that was coming up much too quickly. It would be her first and while she'd talked herself into it, acknowledging that it was an industry requisite for most feature films these days, now that it was swiftly approaching she didn't see how she'd get through it. Not with James Langford. His dangerous reputation with women was well documented but she'd thought she could handle him. She hadn't counted on him being so aggressive.

"Don't remind me," she said before she could get the brakes on.

Getting slowly to his feet he turned to face her, his smile definitely wolfish. "Little Miss Alexandra Martel is a prude. How delightful! It's going to be one steaming hot bedroom scene too, I'll make sure of that. But if I mess up a little there'll be take after take. Some scenes can take almost endless takes. As you know the camera will pick up on even the teeniest bit of tension, so unless you're into it one hundred percent it's going to take us awhile and I for one hope it does."

She swallowed her growing anxiety. A difficult director and now a letch were beginning to turn what could be her big break into a nightmare. She'd thought her generic TV specials, with her clothes on, were challenging enough.

"James, I happen to know you're exaggerating and I want you to leave," she told him evenly. "I have lines to go over and I want to get some sleep. We have an early start in the morning, which I'm sure you haven't forgotten either."

"I hardly need reminding, darlin', I know how it works."

"Soooo...."

"Soooo that's why I'm here, to help you."

"Help me in what way?" she asked, affronted. "Running lines?"

"Not exactly," he said with a smile.

If he knew how to behave properly she would gladly accept input from an actor of his ability and stature, anyone but him. James Langford was pure magic onscreen, proven box office gold, but...."

"Thanks, but no thanks."

"Thanks but no thanks! Alexandra, you haven't seen Nigel in a full-blown freak out yet and I promise you it's something you want to avoid if you can. He's already riding you some because he's not seeing any chemistry between you and me. It's there for me, but you need to do some serious thawing out."

"Get out, James!"

"Sit down, Alexandra," he sighed before taking another pull on his drink. "Your chastity is safe with me, for tonight anyway. Go take that bath sheet off your head, do a comb out and then come back. I think it'll help you relax a little, let some of that tension go. It's no fun for cast or crew if you're continually messing up. Now go on and do as I say, then put on your big girl pants and we'll get into our characters a bit. Get a better feel for tomorrow."

She studied him for a moment, arms now crossed. "You know, James, what you're saying makes perfect sense and I am flattered you'd take the time to help little ole me. It's just that I get the distinct feeling you want more."

"More?"

"I think you want more than a professional relationship."

Draining the contents of his glass before setting it down on the nearby coffee table, he returned his attention to her. "More, you say. Please be so good as to enlighten me, milady," he said with dramatic affect.

She puffed a pent-up sigh. "James, I'm tired."

"Then stop wasting time."

"I mean I don't want to do this."

"What, do some extra work that might improve your performance? You've got a lot to learn if you don't think that's a good idea. All of us need help from time to time."

"I agree with that, I'm talking about the more part of it. You want more than I'm willing to give is what I'm saying. I like to get everything on the table right up front. Manage expectations. You've been coming onto me but you're wasting your time in that regard. I'm only interested in what goes on in front of the cameras between you and I, nothing more."

"I want more, and that's what I've been trying to convey to you, but you want to play hard to get, apparently. Look, I like you, Alexandra. I pushed hard to get you on this film because I think you've got what it takes to go all the way, no pun intended. And you tested well for the part, so don't fall apart now. We're just getting started."

"Something tells me you and Nigel are friends. He seems to go very easy on you."

"Sure we're friends. Nothing wrong with that and he's all for you and I getting together off screen, in case you're interested. You know if you gave it half a chance it could be good, and gee, Alexandra, would we light up that screen when it spilled over from the bedroom. I'm not telling you something you haven't already figured out. Be nice to me and I'll open doors for you. You have no idea how big you could be."

"Do you think I don't know your reputation? I'd only be your flavour of the month. This is like the casting couch in reverse. I already got the part, James, I don't need to sleep with you to get on this film. I'm already here."

He reclaimed the easy chair and settled back before he spoke. "Don't be shortsighted, Alexandra. There's always tomorrow. This isn't the only movie that's ever going to be made. I assume you're in this for the long haul, unless you want to continue to be a big star on a small stage. You look smarter than that so I would suggest you get with the program. You're worried about a little casual sex? It's done all the time, sweetheart. Do you think we'd be the only ones who ever hooked up on a movie shoot? Hardly. It's one big party. Hard work, yes, but we all need to let off steam and I can't think of any better way to go about it than that."

"Go hook up with someone else then, I want to go to bed."

He laughed and she had to admit he even did that well. She couldn't remember when she'd ever seen a more handsome man. He had definitely won the mega lottery when it came to looks, but he was not sexy. Not in her opinion, and therein lay the rub. Not that she'd jump into bed with him under these circumstances if he were. She had more self-respect than that. She had no intention of bed hopping, with anyone.

"You want to go to bed? Then we're on the same page after all. We could do the work I think we should do after we go to bed if that's what you want, or before."

"James, get over yourself. I mean I want to go to bed alone."

"Doesn't sound like much fun to me."

"This is ridiculous. I want you to leave. Then I'm going to dry my hair, go over my lines and try to get some sleep before morning. I don’t want bags under my eyes from lack of sleep.”

“No to the balloon tires as we call them because we’ve got some close-ups tomorrow, but yes to us working together. I’ll be honest with you, Alexandra. Can I call you Alex?”

“No, you can’t. Call me Alexandra,” she replied waspishly, knowing that people often did call her Alex. She just didn’t want to be over-familiar with him.

“All right then, A-l-e-x-a-n-d-r-a. What I was saying is that I am honestly attracted to you, and I want to be with you. What the future holds is anyone’s guess, but I see you and I together for the long haul. What’s so terrible about that? Women are usually flattered by my attention, and this time it’s you.”

“Right. I saw you chatting up one of the production assistants. Where is she tonight? Not able to pick her lock?”

“That’s another thing I like about you, Alexandra is your sense of humour. Okay, you win. No sexy rendezvous tonight, but seriously, it would be beneficial to spend some time working out parts of tomorrow’s scenes. I know you know your lines, but let’s explore our character interaction. Those are key scenes.”

There probably weren't too many women who wouldn't drop at James Langford's feet, but she wasn't one of them. "It'd be a lot easier to relax if you'd behave yourself," she told him bluntly. "Just because you recommended me for this movie, for which I sincerely thank you by the way, doesn't mean I'm your property."

"Yet."

"Ever, but I admit it's a good idea to do what you're suggesting. But first I want to make one thing abundantly clear. You are not to come into my trailer unannounced ever again. That was not cool. Very unprofessional and I don't appreciate it."

He made a mocking sweep. "Guilty as charged. To be honest though I did knock several times and there was no answer. I even tried the doorbell. So like the gentleman I am, I let myself in and waited in the living room."

* * *

They spent the next hour and a half working together and she had to give credit where credit was due. He was a master at his craft and deserved his superstar status, yet here he was taking the time to help her. When he looked into her eyes and spoke his tender lines, it was as real as, well, the real thing. And it wasn't hard to tell he was affected by her, but she could not return the compliment. It was the worst feeling to try to dredge up the required emotion when she felt nothing. The worst part was that if she didn't feel it, neither would the camera or anyone else.

But while there were in fact tender love scenes in this movie, James's character, Hubert Patton, was explosively volatile and some very intense interactions between the two of them lie ahead. She did not dread the physicality though. It was the love scenes that were proving to be such a stumbling block for her. She didn't have much experience with them, in real life or in acting, and it showed. If she could pull this off with him, she deserved an award.

Nevertheless when they were finished she did indeed feel much better about what awaited her tomorrow. If in fact she did please Nigel, and it was anybody's guess if that were even possible, it would have been worth the work she'd put in with James tonight. He had shown her things, provided insights she'd thought she was already aware of, and to think she'd almost turned him down.

When they were done he got up to leave in a most gentlemanly manner, stopping in the doorway. "Alexandra," he said, suddenly serious, "I'm falling in love with you and I'm not going to apologize for that. When you close those big blue eyes of yours tonight to go to sleep, think about what I said earlier about you and me. Goodnight.”

She locked the door behind him, still reeling from his parting declaration. It wasn’t the first time she’d ever heard that but had never taken even one of those actor lotharios seriously. She hadn’t felt genuinely attracted to any co-stars she’d worked with to date, and there’d been some fine looking actors.

In any event it was time for bed, and she’d always been fortunate in that she had a great relationship with sleep. When she asked for it, she was never disappointed, and it came quickly again tonight. The last thoughts before she drifted off were how she’d love to meet someone she’d want to make a commitment to, like her two sisters had: Shane Elliott and Hayden Barlowe. But so far nothing, not even Hollywood hunk James Langford stirred her blood.

* * *

Dawn was beginning to break in peach and apricot splendour when Alexandra’s alarm sprang to life the next morning. Truth to tell she’d come awake before it rang, but it was always nice to have that insurance in case she went over, by a little or a lot. After her later than usual bedtime she was surprised she felt as chipper as she did, but she wouldn’t look a gift horse in the mouth.

The air was sweet and brisk this early in the morning and the songbirds were in full chorus, her windows raised to catch that most welcome serenade. How she loved being back in New Brunswick. She'd missed it. Oh she'd loved seeing other places, the most exotic so far being Ireland, but it was nice to be back here if only for a little while.

Always on a friendly basis with the rest of the cast and crew, she'd be happy to visit the catering truck like everyone else, except that one of the perks she'd requested was her own choice of food.

She didn't mind cooking for herself, and a very early breakfast gave her a chance to eat, shower and have her teeth cleaned before the catering truck even arrived. That meant a little extra time to relax, get into the groove before hair and make-up because the call to set would come early.

"You don't look any the worse for wear," came the familiar voice behind her as she stepped out into the fresh cool air.

She turned to him with a smile. "Hello, James," she said, forcing cheerfulness into her tone.

In all fairness though she felt much more ready to face rehearsal today than she no doubt would have if it hadn't been for James. Learning her lines had never been a problem. She had them down cold, but she must also be ready for anything unplanned, anything that would be beneficial to the movie. It wasn't all done by rote. Sometimes the best moments were the unexpected ones, and a good actor must also be ready for those. It was always good to give the editor plenty to work with. And she could honestly say, after last night, she had a much better feel for her character.

As grateful as she was for this opportunity with Retribution, her mother liked to say there was always a fly in the ointment, in reference to the Biblical proverb. In this case that would be the director. He'd be a challenge even for industry veterans. Add James Langford to the mix and she had to admit that at times she felt a tad overwhelmed. Either one of them alone would be a handful, but two of them on one film were a lot to deal with. Nevertheless she was marching forward into the day with a positive attitude.

"That's it? Hello, James?" he challenged her.

She raised well-shaped eyebrows. "Yes, hello, James."

"How about hello, James, thank you for stopping by last night. That was very nice of you to come to my trailer and spend time working with me."

"How about breaking into my trailer and suggesting we sleep together?" was her pleasant rejoinder.

"Sure, be happy to. Same time as last night?"

She pulled a face. "Very funny. Honestly though, James, working through those scenes with you was very helpful. I do appreciate it. Thank you again."

That seemed to satisfy him for the moment, winking at her before heading off in the opposite direction.

* * *

Following hair and make-up, James was at her elbow as they got into one of the white vans carrying the cast and crew from basecamp to the Fenwick mansion. Sitting on spacious grounds adjacent to scenic Belleisle Bay, the fjord-like arm of the magnificent St. John River, the mansion provided a breathtaking location. It was a spectacular morning and within minutes they arrived and filed into the living room to rehearse the first scene of the day.

Not every director wanted his actors to rehearse, some preferring spontaneity, but Nigel had made it well known he saw rehearsal as valuable time spent with his actors. She had to agree because she liked the back and forth between cast members to make sure they were all on the same page. This scene was a fight between her and James as husband and wife, and it was going to get physical. There were always stunt people if something over the top was called for, but all it would be today was a little push and shove.

Nigel, wearing his director's hat, was in a sour mood and if the uncompromising set of his jaw was anything to go by, his hair trigger temper was in top form. "Alexandra, I've decided I want this scene to be a lot more physical than it calls for in the script."

She gave Nigel her full attention, and although she found it hard to speak up to a director of his stature, in this case a man who seemed to rely on intimidation, she did so anyway. "How physical?"

Nigel's eyes narrowed. "As physical as I say it should be I suppose. How about you, James?"

James thought a moment. "I'm up for that. Who gets slapped the hardest, me or Alexandra?"

Nigel shifted his attention back to her and she couldn't help but think his smile was malicious. "Alexandra of course. I want you to really connect with her, and Alexandra, I want real tears, not the crocodile variety. But that's toward the end of the scene. So I want the argument to escalate naturally, but

James, you'll take a step ahead in order to be positioned to let her have it. I want *everyone* to feel that slap."

Alexandra worked to keep her expression neutral. "Okay, so you say I'm to still slap James, but not as hard. I want to make sure I understand it correctly."

Nigel folded his arms. "You do understand, correctly. Very good!"

Her eyes never left the director's face. "Why is that I wonder?"

She knew as soon as the words left her lips it would be like lighting a fuse on a stick of dynamite and he looked at her ominously. "Because that's the way I want it to be, and the way I want it to be is what is best. Do not question me, Miss Martel. Now, assume your positions and let's walk through it. Not the real thing at the moment, in case you're tempted to get one in at Mr. Langford for whatever reason."

She ignored the remark and both she and James took their positions, choreographing their way through the slap in slow motion. She was not looking forward to the real thing, but she'd prove she could do it. Nigel Garretson was well known for his realism, and this was going to be one of those occasions.

So taking their positions as they would when the cameras were rolling, Alexandra sat on the sofa. James stood over her in a menacing stance, his actions scripted to escalate to physical violence.

Slipping effortlessly into Sari Patton's skin, she felt the isolation of living in a remote location with her unhinged billionaire husband who'd promised her the moon and stars if she'd reconcile with him. As the storyline went, she'd walked out on him because of his bizarre behavior. But she'd been lured back with false promises and was now the victim of what he felt was just retribution. She sat on the sofa with her legs crossed, her head thrown back affecting a cavalier attitude as she embodied the character of Sari.

Nigel studied her position. "Okay now, Miss Martel, I want you to sit up straight, not lounge back like that. It looks as though you're waiting for your next customer at a bordello. Mrs. Patton is not that kind of woman. You'll have to be innovative I suppose, not rely on life experience to guide you."

Alexandra could feel her face redden but wisely held her tongue and sat up straight on the sofa as the director indicated, crossing her legs for a primmer demeanour.

James waited until she was in position. "Okay," he said, glancing at the director, "I've come storming in and am standing over her making threatening gestures."

Nigel nodded. "Precisely, James. Your body language will speak volumes and terrify her all the more. She will be in a state of fear before you even speak. Okay, let's try that."

James held his position while Alexandra remained as directed, feet crossed at the ankles, hands folded in her lap.

Nigel stood watching as James loomed angrily over his movie wife, his hands on his hips, glaring at her.

Nigel nodded. "Okay, that's excellent, James. Perfect. Now Alexandra, you're much too stiff. You're not in church you know. Loosen up a little. Stand up, roll your shoulders a few times and take that strained look off your face. It's very off-putting."

She got up and did as was asked of her. Chances are she did look strained. She felt strained because this movie was already feeling more like a chore than a dream come true. However she must rise above it all and not let true stardom slip away because of Nigel's nastiness. And James had hinted he could open doors for her, although she would not sleep with him for the privilege.

Having rolled her shoulders and made a concerted effort to relax, they rehearsed again, and Nigel seemed content with her performance. Finally it was time to shoot the scene and she hoped sincerely that today would be an improvement over yesterday. And she had that slap to look forward to.

At the end of the day the slap was not the real thing, and she was grateful for that much at least. Nigel had misled her into thinking she'd actually be struck to put her in the correct frame of mind.

* * *

The man checked his watch as he drove the dark SUV up the winding country road. It had been child's play to find where Alexandra was filming Retribution. She'd given that away herself during a recent television interview. She was a stunning young woman and that fact alone attracted media attention. Regrettably his plans to take her had fallen short. He was not at all practiced in this sort of thing. He would get her eventually, it was a matter of time. So far it had proven nearly impossible to find her alone.

It had seemed so simple at the outset with her staying in the middle of nowhere, but there was a lot of hustle and bustle around what was referred to as basecamp. Because of the remoteness of the shoot and lack of suitable hotel space in the area, his research revealed the best and most timely accommodations would be to provide trailers for all and sundry. Gaining access to that area was nearly impossible. He'd almost managed it yesterday until some penny ante security guard asked him who he was and what he wanted. He'd made up some excuse about being lost and hightailed it out of there. So it didn't look like basecamp was going to work out the way he needed it to, but failure was not an option. Time was running out. He needed to make his move soon. His life depended on it.

"Come to me, little one," he said aloud in the cab of the vehicle as though doing so would influence the desired outcome. He'd found a good place to get his vehicle off the road the other day, a very convenient hiding spot so he could watch, familiarize himself with her comings and goings. It seemed she was always with someone, especially travelling in those vans, but sooner or later he'd get his chance. All it would take was one misstep, and he'd have her.

Chapter 2

Beau rolled out of bed at his usual morning start time of four-thirty. That's all the sleep he'd ever needed, and it meshed perfectly with his get up and go attitude. Even if he was inclined to sleep longer, his three dogs, Carley, Ajax and Ron would see to it that his feet hit the floor in time to let them out to answer the call of nature. Ron was his latest rescue, and it was amazing how much he'd improved since he'd found him by the creek a little over two months ago.

The dogs headed for the back door ahead of him, Carley as usual barking in anticipation of open-door freedom. There were squirrels waiting to be chased, although it was never a close contest. In fact he could swear the little squirrel waited for his friend, clinging to the side of the tree, chattering excitedly. It easily scampered to safety high in the branches of the venerable old oak that had seen countless generations of red squirrels.

Beau's usual busy day awaited him at his veterinary clinic at Hatfield Point in the heart of Belleisle. He and his assistant, Hailey Cruickshank, had easily handled the small number of sick or injured animals when he'd first opened, but business had steadily increased until it had become necessary to expand his practice. That's when he'd added Dr. Jennifer Tuttle to his payroll, in addition to a second assistant and a vet tech. That worked out great because Dr. Jen was an absolute gift, picking up the slack when he was needed on farm calls. And now with the movie Retribution being filmed in the area, and he being the veterinarian on call for that production, a larger staff would come in handy.

However, as great as Dr. Jen was turning out to be, it was becoming increasingly obvious she had more than a passing interest in him. Not that she wasn't a wonderful woman, there was simply no interest on his part. A person couldn't manufacture those feelings, there had to be a seed from which it could grow and it just wasn't there. He liked her as a friend but preferred to keep the whole thing on a professional basis. Dr. Jen apparently felt otherwise and although she kept her feelings to herself, it was all right there in her eyes. He'd been trying his best to ignore it so they wouldn't have to have *that* conversation, and he was hopeful she'd lose interest over time.

His thoughts shifted to the movie set he'd soon be visiting, even though his on-set presence wouldn't be required until the wolf dogs were used in a couple of weeks. He'd received the call from production staff months ago because of his specialty in veterinary emergency and critical care, and he was ideally situated in close proximity to the movie location. He'd been reluctant at first to accept because he was already busy enough, but he'd since had more time to consider the opportunity. It might be fun to be part of a motion picture crew, despite how limited that involvement was. All that was required of him was to be on hand to render immediate care in case of any mishaps. It was good to see that animal welfare was top priority. An animal safety representative was present on the set of television shows and movies when necessary, and then there were the trainers and handlers. He'd checked them out for this production. They were some of the best in the business and took very good care of their valuable animals.

He could hear Ajax scratching at the back door, his outside business taken care of and now ready for breakfast.

"Come on in, old boy," Beau laughed. "Breakfast is served," and he indicated Ajax's bowl with a sweep of his hand before breaking eggs into a frying pan where bacon was already sizzling for his own meal.

His thoughts returned to the movie, a definite one-off. Belleisle wasn't exactly the film capital of the world, but he could see why the area's stunning natural beauty would be an enticement. Whatever, he only had a passing interest in the entertainment industry. He didn't even own a television set and had zero interest in doing so. Nope, a good book was what he enjoyed at the end of a long hard day and there was always professional material to keep abreast of. That being said, if he had any free time today he should go up to where they were filming and have a look around, kind of get acquainted with the whole thing before he was called to set.

The strident ringing of the telephone jolted him from his thoughts.

"Hi, Dr. Remington, it's Nancy Sweet."

"Just Beau," he reminded the new veterinary assistant pleasantly.

She giggled nervously. "I'm afraid we have an emergency, Beau. A dog was found this morning, and I was told he's just skin and bones. The guys who're bringing him in don't think he's going to make it, but they're coming anyway. They said they'll be here in about an hour."

He was instantly alert. "What are the circumstances? They think he was deliberately starved?"

"Not from what they said. Apparently Old Ned was a hermit who lived in a shack way back in the woods. No one had seen him around for a while, so they went to check up on him, and he's dead. They also found his dog and he was starving. It had been chained up so couldn't forage for itself."

Beau swore under his breath, he could only imagine the suffering of that poor animal. "I'll be right along as soon as I finish up here. I should be there by the time they arrive. Thanks, Nancy."

Beau gobbled down his bacon and eggs, skipped toast and coffee and headed for the barn where he turned out his horses, put enough hay in the feeders for the day and filled the water tubs. He'd clean their stalls when he came back later. The dogs had already eaten so he put them in the compound with plenty of drinking water. He'd built the chain link canine enclosure himself, providing a spacious run and lots of cool shade during summer heat with comfy beds to curl up on. Carley was the puppy of the trio at four years old, while Ajax and Ron were over ten and well into their sunset years. Comfort was the key word for all of them, and they had that in spades with Beau. After giving Ajax and Ron their medication he grabbed a quick shower, jumped in his pick-up truck and headed for the clinic.

Now with eight years of practicing veterinary medicine to his credit, Beau knew he shouldn't be shocked anymore at what came through his door. To anyone who had a genuine love for animals, every case of trauma was upsetting. You never got past that. The difference was the ability to rise above it and do what needed to be done to try to save a life.

* * *

Ten minutes after he arrived at the clinic the emaciated dog was carried inside. He was told his name was Barney, and when the animal recognized his name he weakly wagged his tail.

"I remember this dog," said Felix Miller, who along with his brother Royden had gone to check up on Ned. "Old Ned got him when he was still a pup, I'd say about two or three years ago. He fed him scraps and stuff, but he was never what you'd call a big dog."

Beau nodded before waving the men forward. "Okay, bring him right in and lay him on the table," he said, pointing to the stainless steel examining table. "Thank you for your help, now we need to get to him right away. If we don't do something fast, we might lose him. He's severely malnourished."

Barney made no sound as Felix laid him gently on the table, then left to join his

brother in the waiting room. Before leaving the clinic to go with the RCMP back to Old Ned's place, both men asked to be contacted regarding the dog's progress and generously offered to pay for his care.

Back in the examining room the dog looked up at Beau with imploring eyes, his whole body trembling and offering no resistance as his physical exam began. Barney remained silent as Beau checked him over from nose to tail, not showing any sign of pain when he palpated his abdomen. As he expected though his pale gums and tongue were definitely cause for concern.

Not surprisingly Barney was badly dehydrated, but when he was given a small amount of water he did try to lap at it and that was a hopeful sign.

"It's okay, Barney," said Hailey as she gently stroked the dog's forehead. "We're going to get you all fixed up, sweetie."

Beau nodded. "Okay, we need a complete CBC/Chemistry profile and urinalysis. We also have to do a fecal test, check for parasite nasties and see what else is going on there."

"Absolutely," Hailey agreed, all business. "Okay, Barney," she said turning her attention to the dog, "we have to do a bit more poking but we're going to make you well."

"I'll have Nancy give Paulette Nowlan a call to see if she's available to foster this little guy if he doesn't require hospitalization," said Beau. "She's had great success with refeeding. I don't think she's lost one yet that she's worked to bring back. Patience is always key, and Paulette is the soul of patience. I'd say that ole Barney here will need to be dewormed and for sure he needs to be defleaed, but we'll take care of his more immediate needs first."

The results were forthcoming within the hour. Miraculously, other than worms and fleas, Barney was in remarkably good shape for having lived most of his life on the end of a chain. He'd existed on food scraps until even that source of nourishment was gone.

Beau ruffled Barney's coat affectionately. "He's also going to need probiotics and vitamins and I'd say this little mutt will make a full recovery. Did someone get hold of Paulette?"

Hailey smiled, "She came right down when we called her and is sitting in the waiting room. She's anxious to meet Barney and get him started on your refeeding plan."

"Okay, we're going to try Barney on Optimum Diet for puppies. That's highly digestible and meat-based, so grab the five kg bag of that, and also put together those supplements I've made a note of. You can bring Paulette in to meet Barney now and when she's ready to speak to me, I'll be in my office. Thanks, Hailey."

"Sure thing, Beau."

He took care of two telephone messages that needed to be dealt with and had just finished with the second call when there was a tap on the door and Paulette Nowlan stuck her head in.

"Come on in, Paulette," he beckoned to her. "Glad to hear you've got room for another foster. You've got a good track record with refeeding and Barney is going to need your expert TLC."

"The only fur people I'm fostering at the moment are a pair of kittens found on the side of the road. It's a bad time of the year for that. I'm looking forward to taking care of little Barney. I understand his owner was found deceased."

"Yep, he'd been gone for some time apparently and that's why his dog is in the condition he is. I hate to see an animal chained because if anything goes wrong they can't fend for themselves. But even though Barney is in decent shape physically, I'll be sending deworming medication and flea treatment home with you. How many dogs have you brought back to health now? Quite a few I think."

Paulette, now well into her sixties would have made an excellent veterinarian. "This little fellow will make ten. It takes time and patience as you know and he's young, so that's in his favour. It shouldn't be a problem at all to find a new home for him when he's ready to go to one."

Beau smiled. "You amaze me, Paulette, that you're able to find such good homes for the animals you work with."

"I keep my feelers out all the time and I get plenty of calls from people asking me if I'm fostering an animal, you know people looking to adopt. The two kittens that I've affectionately named Fuzz and Fuzzette are going to a good home in Springfield. As you know, before I let any of my babies go I always check out who's doing the asking. I almost got burned once when I was fostering a batch of kittens. A man called and said he'd take all five, but as it turned out he had a boa constrictor, and I don't have to tell you why he made such a generous offer."

"You've had great success with the dogs we've sent you over the years. It's not an easy job to renourish an emaciated dog. Refeeding syndrome is very real. Not many people realize that if they're fed too much too soon the dog's system, already compromised, will be overwhelmed."

"Slow and easy is key, and they love their mid-morning and mid-afternoon snacks, especially cheese and chicken. Every mouthful I give them does my heart good. I say they do more for me than I ever could do for them. I love them all."

"Beau shook his head. "You're a wonder and we're very lucky to have you, Paulette. Keep up the good work."

* * *

The rest of the morning went as expected. He had to neuter John Trimbley's cat at ten o'clock, and Pearl Simcoe's dog at eleven-fifteen. Both surgeries were routine, but they were anything but that to their loving owners. The level of love an owner had for their pet could never be underestimated. He made a point to meet with both John and Pearl before their animals were released, making sure they were provided with the proper pain medication and post-surgical instructions.

Before noon he saw Caitlyn Dashwood's twenty-pound cat and if ever there was a feisty feline, Snowdrop was it. Cantankerous and not afraid to show it, Snowdrop was one angry dude and without a protective muzzle he could easily cause physical injury. Hailey had already made one trip to the hospital thanks to Snowdrop's aggressiveness. If there was one thing in the entire world that

Snowdrop detested it was a visit to the vet for his annual examination and needling. Other than that his owner had assured Beau he was as docile as a lamb.

Some veterinarians would refuse to treat such a difficult pet, but the way he saw it, most animals could be worked with. It took patience as well as careful management.

* * *

It was a little after three o'clock when he left the office to drive up to the movie set. He'd already met with the director a couple of months ago when he and the location manager had come to the area to scout out a suitable setting for Retribution. He recalled that Nigel Garretson was excited to find what he had envisioned for his movie when he saw the New Brunswick informal geographic region of Belleisle, situated as it was on scenic Belleisle Bay. The cherry on top was the Fenwick Mansion, the summer home of wealthy financier Drew Fenwick and his family. It fitted the storyline to a tee. By a stroke of good fortune the property was available because the Fenwicks were summering at Cape Cod this year.

Beau started up the long graveled drive that led to the mansion, but he hadn't gone very far before he was met by a uniformed security guard who demanded to see his pass. Of course he had one, but the guy acted as though he'd been caught trying to breach the perimeter of the Royal Canadian Mint. But then again he supposed, one never knew who might lurking around. He had to admit there was an inviting mystique about moviemaking that drew people in and if one of them happened to be a nut, then this level of response was understandable.

"Good afternoon, sir," the young man relented once he saw he wasn't dealing with an infidel. "Drive on down and pull your vehicle off to the side where everyone else is parked and wait. They're in the middle of shooting right now, but they could be free within an hour or so. I guess it depends on how well it goes."

"No problem," Beau told him. "I don't mind waiting for a while."

"Very good, my man," the guard responded, as though he was part of the actual movie crew or should have been given his level of devotion. He was a member of the overall team and accordingly colourful.

It was a hot day with not even a slight breeze to stir the surrounding countryside and Beau was glad of his vehicle's air conditioning. He might even treat himself to a dip in the bay tonight to cool off. He'd take the dogs with him. They were always good for a splash or two, fetching a stick and that sort of thing. Poor old Ajax was so full of arthritis now he'd watch from the shoreline, cheer the others on. Beau figured too that young Chance might like to stretch *his* legs a bit, so he might even go for a ride later.

His three horses, one rescue and two surrenders, all had the same name oddly enough, and that was Chance. And what were the chances of that seeing as how in his experience most of the Chances he'd met were dogs. In any event he'd left their names as they were, and they didn't seem a bit confused when he called for Chance. They came to the name, all he had to do was look at the horse he was speaking to, and the rest was straightforward.

The oldest Chance was a twenty-four-year-old black found abandoned in a pasture. He'd been in relatively good shape and responded immediately to veterinary care. The second Chance was a Palomino mare, about eighteen he guessed, and then there was eight year-old Chance, a sleek dark chestnut gelding whose owner had decided she "wasn't into horses anymore."

Beau rode all three, although young Chance saw the most trail time. He'd needed to put a little more training on the young chestnut to correct some bad habits, but he'd learned fast and was a very giving animal. The Palomino and the black were quiet pleasure horses while the youngster of the bunch gave Beau the spirited, high-octane ride he enjoyed. There was nothing quite like a spirited animal and he knew that young Chance understood when Beau climbed in the saddle he expected to have a little lightning under him.

Beau had participated in cattle penning and gymkhana growing up on a ranch in the rural community of Jemseg. He'd enjoyed his time with those equine sports, even if he'd more or less stepped away from it all when he went off to university. And then he'd been too darned busy to take them up again, although he rode whenever he got the opportunity. It was something that came second nature to him. He'd been in the saddle by the time he was three, his dad the ideal hands-on father. As an only child there was no shortage of attention from his parents, and he treasured all the happy childhood memories they'd given him. Both of his parents were accomplished horse people with an impressive trophy room to show for their prowess.

There had always been the subtle expectation that he'd move back to the ranch when he'd completed his education. However it was that same pioneer spirit that saw his parents build the Wind Song Ranch that meant he too wanted to strike out on his own, somewhere else. He was determined to start a veterinary clinic. He hadn't gone far, only about forty kilometres down the road, but he was proud of what he'd accomplished so far.

Deep in thought, he jumped when there was a rap on his driver's window. It was the same security guard.

"Excuse me, sir," the young man said once Beau had rolled down the glass. "I've heard the shoot is almost over and the director should be free within the hour if you want to continue to wait."

Beau shrugged. "No problem. I'm kind of enjoying the downtime."

"Sure thing. I'll get word inside that you're waiting to see him and hopefully you two can connect before too much longer."

"You're saying they'll be done for the day in a little while?"

"Oh no, they'll go on for some time yet. It's usually early evening before they call it a day, and then the cast and crew go to supper. Security stays here all night to guard the property and sets."

Beau nodded. "That's understandable. Can I get out of my vehicle and walk around a bit?"

"Absolutely. Clip your pass to your pocket to avoid being hassled, and don't go anywhere you're not supposed to. I'd say you could take a walk down by the water if you want. The grounds are really great and they're not shooting anything down that way at the moment. It's all inside the mansion for the next couple of days I understand. I make it my business to know a lot about how things work."

Beau smiled. "That right?"

"Yep. You're looking at a future star, right here. I'm going to get into movies some day and make it big. I won't be working for minimum wage as a security guard. Nosiree."

Beau nodded thoughtfully. You couldn't fault the guy's enthusiasm, and what was wrong with dreaming big? "I wish you all the luck in the world."

The guard did have an engaging smile, and now that the ice had been broken he was talkative and friendly. "That's always been my dream. When I heard there were openings on their security team I applied right away. It's a very big deal to even be this close to the whole thing. I'm drinking everything in because you have to start somewhere."

"You act do you?" asked Beau, making conversation.

The kid shook his head. "Not yet but I'm going to get into it. I tell you, my man, the fuse has been lit and I'm raring to go. I should have tried to be one of the extras on the show, but I understand they have everyone they need now. So I missed out there, but it won't happen again. My name is Lucas Roberstone and I want you to remember the day you talked to me and what I told you. Then you can say, oh, I remember that guy. He was a security guard on Retribution, and now look at him."

Beau smiled, impressed with the kid's passion. "I'll remember that, Lucas."

Lucas looked around sharply as though talking to Beau was a serious dereliction of duty, in spite of the fact that no one had arrived or left in the past hour and a half.

He returned his attention to Beau. "You know you should think about getting into the movies yourself. You got the face and build for it. How tall are you?"

Beau almost laughed. This was entertaining. "I'm six-two and a half."

"How much do you weigh?"

"About two hundred, give or take. You'd make a good casting director."

"Nah, I'm going for the big bucks, but seriously, you're in great shape for your age. How old are you, thirty ... forty?"

"Thirty-five and I have no interest at all in getting into the movies."

"You already have a job?"

Beau's smile tugged at the corners of his mouth. "Like I said when I came in, I'm the vet hired to work on this picture."

"Vet? As in army veteran?"

"Vet as in veterinarian. So I've already got a gig but thank you for the encouragement. If that doesn't work out I'll consider taking up acting."

"Right. Oh, I see people coming off the set so they must be taking a break. I'd get on over there if you want to catch the director between scenes. Been a pleasure talking to you."

"The pleasure's all mine," said Beau, "and good luck," but the guy was already marching back to his post.

Beau headed in the direction of people spilling out of the mansion and was about to climb the stairs when he came face to face with a gorgeous actress. She had dark hair and crystal blue eyes. Obviously she was one of the stars. He knew he shouldn't be staring, which could rightly be called ogling, but he'd never had such a punch in the gut reaction to a woman, ever.

Their eyes held for what seemed like forever. He was aware he was still staring, and it seemed she was equally as mesmerized although he couldn't understand why. He'd been described by women in the past as ruggedly handsome, but he was no pretty boy movie star. He was suddenly aware of his T-shirt, jeans and boots because he dressed as he pleased wherever he went. He was not a television version of what a vet should look like.

She was dressed in fine clothes, her hair arranged off her face in an elegant upsweep

They appeared to be complete opposites, but it seemed neither one could look away.

Chapter 3

She extended her hand. "I'm Alexandra Martel," she told him, her eyes never leaving his face.

He took her hand and perhaps held onto it a moment too long before squeezing it in a gesture of greeting then letting it go. "Beau Remington," he said as he noticed her checking out his ID badge, and his ring finger.

Her eyes widened slightly. "Dr. Remington? You're a doctor? Is someone sick?"

He smiled, aware that it warmed his face considerably because he'd often been told he should do it more often. "Not that kind of doctor," he assured her, "and to the best of my knowledge there's no medical emergency on set. I'm a veterinarian. I'll be here in case one of the animals that'll eventually be used in the movie gets injured. It's only a precautionary measure. I'm sure everything will be fine. Still, you never know. I'll also be observing the animals to see if they're showing any signs of abuse. I know there are others here to monitor the same thing, but I'll be watching for that as well.

"I don't agree with animals being used for entertainment because I've read some horror stories about fear-based training, horrendous living conditions and the rest. But the Harmonds own five wolf hybrids as pets and those animals have a great quality of life on their spread down in Maine. They're trained to appear on film, but that's not their principal purpose in life. It's only a secondary thing. Anyway, that's why I'm here."

She laughed and it made her eyes dance. "I'm certainly glad I talked to you! I feel much better now. I have to admit when I saw they were using wolf dogs I was uncomfortable. What do you know about the breed? I get they're part wolf and part dog, but that's about it."

"There's a lot to say about them but the first word that comes to mind is their personalities can be unpredictable, especially early on because dogs and wolves mature at different rates. It's like a blending of wild and domestic, and their behavior can be challenging at times because there's still a lot of wild in them."

Her eyes widened, an ocean of crystal blue. "Do you think we'll be safe around them?"

"How extensive is your interaction with them?"

"It's like a simulated attack but I don't think I get too close. I have to pet one of them at some point, but I don't usually have a problem with big dogs. I'm not terrified or anything."

"There are two wolf hybrids in this movie and like I say I already checked out the owners/trainers and they're the best of the best. They understand the breed and that at least half of their genetic make-up is wild wolf and can manage their behavior accordingly. But you also have to take into consideration there are now multi generations of wolf dogs bred to wolf dogs. So there's that aspect of it too with owners who say they're no different than any other dog. Anyway, the Harmond brothers are highly educated about wolf dogs, so I'd say you're in good hands."

"I'm guessing they're aggressive though."

"They can be very aggressive under certain circumstances. Much of it is fear motivated, but a movie set is a very controlled atmosphere and those trainers, who understand any potential complications of the wolf/dog cross, are totally equipped to handle them. Again, I'm not here because there's a concern that anyone working with them could be attacked, it's in case the animals themselves get injured which again is not likely. Your director is covering all of his bases, and I'm guessing he wants to avoid the potential landslide of negative publicity if he did any part of this improperly. So you're going to pat them a little?"

"There's only one scene when one of them comes up to me, but they're in the room with me on a couple of occasions."

"Don't worry, their trainers will be with them on set. I've seen pictures of the hybrids and they're superb looking animals. They'll look good on film. The director will get his shots, but he'll do it in a safe way for both the actors and the animals."

She laughed. "I know the welfare of the animals are being looking after. Because this is a US movie production the American Humane Association rep will be present and then there's you too in case something goes wrong. So win/win, right?"

He smiled again, which he found himself doing easily these past few minutes. "Win/win. Absolutely."

He was sure he'd never seen a more alluring woman. He'd had his share of dalliances in the past, but even at thirty-five he was still not in any hurry to settle down, much to the consternation of his parents who were chomping at the bit for grandchildren. Maybe he was turning out to be a confirmed bachelor. He'd almost gotten hitched to Melody Parnell a few years ago, but he'd come to his senses in time to put the brakes on. Melody was a great girl, loads of fun, but she liked to party a little too much and in the end he'd known their relationship wouldn't work long term. But this Alexandra Martel interested him right off the bat.

He kept his eye out for the director but so far hadn't seen him emerge from the building. He should go see if he could find him, but Alexandra was much more interesting to look at and talk to.

"So you're from the US are you, Alexandra?" loving the way her name rolled off his tongue. So sexy.

She shook her head. "I'm from New Brunswick. I mean I was born in Toronto, but I grew up in Franklin, which is less than an hour away. So this is great for me to be back in the province for a while."

Now that was a surprise! "Oh! You must live in the US though if you're on an American movie location."

Again she shook her head, and he'd bet if that long dark hair of hers was loose it would tumble well past her shoulders. "I live in Toronto. The male lead for this movie, James Langford, lives in California. He saw me in my last production and wanted me for this movie. What James Langford wants, James Langford usually gets so they tested me for the female lead but chose another actress. Anyway, to make a long story short I ended up getting the part. James can be very persuasive."

Now that wasn't necessarily good news. He could only imagine most men would want her attention. If this big deal actor wanted her for the female lead, and she got the part, he must really be invested and in all probability more than just professionally.

Her eyes sparkled. "I'm very impressed that you're a veterinarian. That must be a very interesting career. Do you work with small animals or big ones?"

"Both big and small, but my specialty is emergency and critical care and that covers them all. I don't work with exotic species though. I thought about it for a while, maybe see some of the world working in zoos and stuff, but at the end of the day I decided I would rather stay around these parts."

"Do you have your own practice?"

"Yep, been at it now for a few years. I work with another vet and things can get quite busy at times."

"I think it would be a fascinating line of work. Any emergencies, say today for example?"

He nodded, feeling like the luckiest man alive that he was getting to talk this woman. "This morning we saw a dog whose owner died and there was no one around to feed him."

Her brow furrowed in genuine concern. "You mean he was starving?"

He nodded in the affirmative. "That's right and he was quite emaciated when they brought him in. But we expect him to make a full recovery, so happy ending."

Beau noticed a man come striding toward them, scowling. "Alexandra, the van is waiting to take you back to basecamp. You're holding up the entire crew."

She coloured but stood her ground. "James, I'd like you to meet the veterinarian who'll be on set when the animals are being used. This is Dr. Beau Remington. Dr. Remington this is James Langford."

Langford glanced briefly at Beau. "Yes, the vet. Now come on, Alexandra. Let's get going."

Her face a deep scarlet, she apologized to Beau, explaining she did indeed have to leave, then walked away with the man in the direction of the van. He couldn't help but watch her as she left. Not only was she beautiful, but tall and elegant and she took her leave in long, graceful strides. Minutes later the van pulled out of the yard and made its way toward the entrance. Smiling, she raised her hand to him as they passed.

The van had no sooner left than he spied the director exiting the front door of the mansion and hurried to catch up to him. He'd done his research about Nigel Garretson too and from everything he could see, the director was temperamental and combative with his actors and crew, and prone to histrionics. But he seemed in good humour now as he extended his hand politely.

"It's such a lovely day I'm going to take a walk down to the boathouse, Dr. Remington," he told Beau. "Why don't we walk together, I have a few minutes to spare."

Beau shrugged. "Sure, why not? And you're right, it is a nice day."

They walked down the wide cobblestone path to the shoreline, and during their few minutes together they talked shop about the animals and how Beau should conduct himself on set. That meant basically staying in the background and observing what amounted to commonsense etiquette, but it was still good to have this conversation.

Fifteen minutes later Garretson was headed back to the mansion and Beau to his vehicle when he noticed James Langford had returned and was hurrying to intercept him. He'd seen the actor before in supermarket gossip magazines. He had to say those pictures didn't do the guy justice, and now here was the superstar himself striding toward him. It was one of those days.

"Excuse me, Dr. Remington," said James, frowning.

"Call me, Beau. That's fine."

"Dr. Remington," said James ignoring Beau's attempt to be cordial. "I want to have a little chat with you about Alexandra Martel."

Beau stopped in his tracks, knowing this was not going to be a friendly exchange. The other man obviously had an axe to grind and was determined to get down to it. He turned to face the actor. "What about Alexandra Martel?"

"What about her! Stay away from her, that's what about. She's already spoken for, pal. It's not your job to come here and try to pick up women. Your job is to be on set for the animals. Period."

Beau stared at him. "Are you finished?"

"Not by a long shot. One word from me and all of this goes away."

"All of what?"

"I can get you fired from the set. We can find ourselves another vet in a heartbeat."

Beau shrugged. "Do it then. Go ahead."

James looked surprised. "You're willing to let your big chance slip away just like that?"

Beau laughed, he couldn't help it. "Big chance at what? This?" he asked, glancing around.

"This is moviemaking, my friend. It's not everyday an opportunity like this comes along. Don't blow it."

Now this was getting downright enjoyable. "Are you serious right now?"

"Very serious. I can understand this is no doubt the best thing that's ever happened in your life, but you need to remember it's strictly a hands-off experience. You do the job you were hired to do and that's it."

"Hands off? Let's hope there aren't any accidents or injuries to the animals then."

James' eyes narrowed. "I don't have time for wise guys like you, besides, we weren't using any animals today so why are you even here? Hmmm, oh right. You're here to see if you can get a look at Alexandra Martel and you got lucky. I suppose that means you'll be hanging around from now on trying to get close to her."

Beau cocked his head, folding his arms as he listened. It was obvious Langford felt some sort of entitlement to his leading lady, but what they had going on was no concern of his. To each their own, let them have at it.

"Listen, Mr. Langford," he said, his hands now resting loosely on his hips, "if you're with her that's no skin off my nose. You're right, I'm here to do a job and I have no intention of interfering where I'm not wanted. But the impression I got was she seemed like she was available and by that I mean not spoken for. I'm just sayin'."

James squared his shoulders. "For your information Alexandra is *not* available. She *is* spoken for. As a matter of fact we're engaged."

Beau knew the other guy was making it up as he went along, although it was glaringly obvious he was interested in her. "Engaged?"

"Engaged as in there's going to be a wedding."

"Where was her ring?"

"Naturally she can't wear it on set, but she has it all right. We're going to set a date when this production wraps up. So take my advice and back off. Get on with whatever it is you do all day out here in the sticks."

Beau had a good mind to walk away from this whole movie thing because it was definitely not for him. But then again he hadn't expected to encounter Alexandra Martel and that was purely serendipitous as far as he was concerned. And this cock of the walk strutting around announcing that Alexandra was his, was ridiculous. Never mind what this guy was saying, he and Alexandra had connected. He'd felt it and he was pretty sure she had too, and he knew one thing for sure. He would not be able to get her out of his mind easily, or at all. The waves Langford was trying to create didn't even make his radar.

Beau's cellphone vibrated. It was Hailey from the clinic. "I've got to take this," he told the actor who looked as though he had a lot more he wanted to say, and that proved to be the case when he stood waiting with arms folded, his colour still high.

"Hey, Hailey, what's up?"

"Is it possible for you to come back, Beau? We've got a situation here. Mrs. Calvert was walking her German shepherds and a car ploughed into them. The guy wasn't paying attention or something and went right into them. They've taken Mrs. Calvert to the hospital by ambulance but I understand she wasn't badly hurt. She was talking to them at the scene and she's very worried about her dogs. Both animals have injuries, and they were brought in just as I was calling you. One of the dogs, the female, has a fractured femur. Dr. Jen is already assessing the worst of the two, but we need help."

"I'm on my way," he said as he started to run for his truck. "I'll be there in a few minutes." Ending the call he shoved the phone in his back pocket.

James started after him. "Hey, where are you going? I'm not done talking to you."

"We're done," said Beau as he got into his pick-up, fired it to life and turned to go.

James positioned himself in front of the truck, effectively blocking Beau's path.

"Get out of the way!" Beau told him, his jaw set. "I've got a veterinary emergency."

James had the good sense to step aside but was still dangerously close as Beau accelerated for the entrance. He could hear James shout: "I'll get you fired for trying to run me down!"

"Jerk", Beau said to himself as he raised his hand to the security guard before he made it to the main road and headed for the clinic.

* * *

As it turned out Mrs. Calvert's injuries were thankfully minor, mostly cuts and bruises. The older shepherd, Tolley, had a broken leg and bruising and the younger of the two dogs, Ranson, suffered a dislocated hip and internal injuries that had to be treated surgically. It seemed all three would make a good recovery and everyone in the community breathed a huge sigh of relief. The driver of the vehicle admitted to being distracted while texting.

* * *

Alexandra stretched out on her bed once back in the blessedly cool interior of her luxury trailer, a star wagon as the trailers of principal actors were called. It was her habit now to put chairs under both doorknobs to prevent any more unexpected visits from a certain movie star who thought he was irresistible to women everywhere. Well not to this woman. Even if there had been an attraction to him it disappeared when she laid eyes on Dr. Remington, Beau as he'd insisted she call him. Now there was a bona fide hunk if ever she saw one. She'd seen her share of handsome men, working in the industry as she did, and some had even made her take a second look, but she hadn't been able to take her eyes off Beau Remington.

66

Everything was perfect about the man. She liked his nonchalance for one thing. He seemed quintessentially laidback with a charming sense of quiet confidence. There was something she felt irresistibly drawn to. Not at all a pretty boy, he was a man who gave every impression he could take care of himself in any situation.

She smiled as she picked up her phone and Googled him, and there he was, Dr. Beau Remington, veterinarian at the Hatfield Point Animal Hospital. What a noble profession, helping animals. She adored animals and would love to have a pet, even a small one in her high-rise apartment in Toronto but it was forbidden. And her lifestyle was such that it wouldn't be fair to the animal with her being away so much. No, someday she'd have a pet she thought, lots of them. But that someday was a long way off.

Acting excited her, but even though there were some days when the bloom was off the rose. Dealing with Nigel Garretson and the completely self-absorbed James Langford were not fun, but she was doing what she wanted to do. There was something exhilarating about working on a movie set, as long and demanding as the hours were, and sometimes the people.

She rolled over onto her side, still holding her phone, smiling, and then remembered how rude James had been to

Beau earlier. She hoped her friendly wave as the van left helped mitigate any damage that had been done. Ahhh, James. She thought about yesterday's slapping incident. There'd been something in his eyes when he'd pretended to strike her, that spoke volumes about the man. He'd enjoyed it. He was a talented actor and had not gotten to where he was in Hollywood by not being convincing, but this was different. That glint in the eye either said he thought she had it coming, or it excited him to do violence. Even if she did have any interest in him other than on screen, it would have died in that moment. James Langford was not a nice man. A winner at the box office for sure, but that was it.

She thought about the upcoming film, Twice Dead in the Sullivan At Large franchise, and wondered how she was ever going to stand him for what promised to be a much longer shoot than this one. That is if he even followed through on his recommendation of her for the female lead. Chances were his ardour would have cooled by then anyway and he'd be chasing another pretty face.

She refreshed her screen and brought Beau's website up again. His picture wasn't there, he didn't strike her as the type who needed to have his face, as good looking as it was, plastered all over the place. Not like James Langford.

A broad smile crept slowly into place. For two cents she'd call him she thought wickedly and see what his reaction would be. But no, that would not be the right thing to do. But it's the twenty-first century, she reminded herself unnecessarily. Women *do* call men and again she considered it, but nah. Better to leave it alone. 'What if you never see him again?' she asked herself. Ten to one James had already been busy beating his chest and warning Beau off unless she missed her guess entirely. Still, if she was going to do something like call him, it could wait awhile. Besides, she might see him on set again, and she desperately wanted to.

Her phone rang, startling her and she saw it was her sister, Naomi. "Hey, Naomi," she answered cheerfully. "How are you feeling?"

"Hayden and I went today for my second ultrasound, and drum roll please, we're having a boy. We're both so excited and we're already picking out names, can you believe it?"

"Naomi! I'm so happy for you and Hayden! That's wonderful. Ginger must be happy too."

"She is. Little Heather is growing like a weed. I think she's going to be tall like her mummy and daddy."

"So are you two still planning to come up tomorrow?"

"You bet! We're looking forward to being on a real movie location."

"You'll be visiting me in my trailer I'm afraid. I'm not needed until about noontime, so that's when I'll be heading over to the actual set. But we'll still have a chance to see each other which will be very cool."

"Are you planning to take time off when this movie is done?"

Alexandra sighed. "I want to, need to, but we'll see. I'm hoping that end of it works out. How is Gram doing? You said she was having some trouble with her breathing the last time we talked."

"She got checked and it turns out she had walking pneumonia, but they cleared that up and she's back to her old self. I can tell you one thing too, her first great-grandchild is the apple of her eye, and you should see Shane dote on his little girl. As you know Shane's a serious guy, but he can't keep a grin off his face when he's with the baby. He lights up every time he sees her."

"And Hayden will make a good father too, no question about it. What are some of the names you're thinking about?"

"We both like the name Beau."

Alexandra burst out laughing.

"What's so funny?" Naomi wanted to know. "Beau is a good name, even though Beau Barlowe doesn't quite roll off the tongue, so we'll have to go with something else."

Alexandra was smiling from ear to ear. "I happen to think Beau is a great name, Sis."

Naomi hesitated. "Okay give, you can't fool me. I can see the expression on your face when you say that name, hear it in your voice. Do tell, is there a Beau in your life by any chance?"

Alexandra was enjoying herself. "No, not at all. I've met a Beau is all, and he was every bit as gorgeous as that name sounds."

"Oh? Now you've got me curious. A fellow actor by any chance?"

"Not at all. He's a vet who's hired to be on set when we use the animals in the movie. I met him and thought he was good looking, but that's the extent of it I promise you. I'm sure he's used to women falling all over him but it's hard not to appreciate a hunk when you meet one."

"You're in the right line of work for that, Sis. Anyway, I'll let you go and we'll see you tomorrow morning."

"Great. My assistant will let security know and even though I'm not required on set first thing, that could change. It might turn out to be a short visit. I know it's early to ask you to come, what with Ginger and the baby, and you pregnant, but if you could be here around eight-thirty that would be perfect."

* * *

The man watched from the trees, but the entrance was secure with no less than three guards on duty tonight. It was a matter of opportunity, and he had to be ready to capitalize on it when it came. He took a deep breath to settle his nerves, adrenalin pumping through him.

Chapter 4

Alexandra was so excited the next morning she couldn't even think about breakfast, foregoing her usual bagel with cream cheese. She was about to see her sisters in person for the first time in much too long. They kept in touch through telephone conversations as well as virtual visits via computer, but nothing could compare with in person face-to-face and a warm body to hug.

Her assistant dropped by about seven-thirty to inform her the director wished to meet with her at nine-thirty, so that gave them at least an hour to catch up before she'd be whisked away by van to where an unfailingly punctual Nigel Garretson would be waiting.

At five to eight there came a knock to her door, and she knew instinctively it was Ginger and Naomi even though they were earlier than expected. It was a triplet thing. It could have been James Langford, but to his credit he had not put in an appearance since the night they'd worked on those scenes together. As much as he turned her off, she reminded herself again how hugely beneficial that session had turned out to be.

She answered the door and there stood her sisters, all smiles, Naomi quite obviously pregnant.

"Come in!" she shrieked. "It's so wonderful to see you both."

All three sisters hugged and wiped tears of happiness at being together again.

Alexandra patted Naomi's sixth-month baby bump. "You're starting to pop out there, Sis, but you look marvelous. So healthy! Pregnancy suits you I must say."

Naomi's smile stretched from ear to ear. "Hayden thinks so too and has promised to keep me this way for the next few years. That's why multiples would be good. That way I could get it all over with at once, but in the meantime let's just say I'm well taken care of. Hayden barely lets me out of his sight. He dotes on me day and night. I've never seen a man so happy." She looked at Ginger. "Unless it's Shane. Both of them are completely devoted to us."

Ginger looked around at the interior. "Wow, this is some trailer. Very nice! Are you all staying in trailers? There are quite a few of them, it's like a village in here."

Alexandra nodded. "Since this is a remote location, this is how they house everyone. I'll bet you thought the grounds would be a little more picturesque. I understand this was once a farm and so this big field made the perfect spot for basecamp as they call it. We take a van over to where most of the filming is being done, and you should see the mansion. Unfortunately I can't take you there."

Naomi rested her hands atop her baby bump. "Can we see it from the road?"

Alexandra shook her head. "No, it's down a long lane toward the bay and they have security posted at the entrance."

Ginger nodded. "There was plenty of security at the entrance to this place too. It was so funny when they saw us. The look on one guy's face was priceless. I didn't think he wanted to believe me when I told him there were three of us. If Naomi and I hadn't been together he'd think it was you playing a prank."

Alexandra grinned. "Gee, Ginger, you could stay for a while and do the scene with James Langford. I've got a copy of the script if you want to give it a go. I'm sure you'd do fine because you acted a bit in high school too."

Ginger chuckled. "Acted up you mean, and thanks anyway but no to acting in your movie. They'd soon notice it wasn't you, even if we do all look the same. You're the movie star of the family. I'm quite happy being a writer/office manager. Very happy indeed." She leaned in a little closer. "So what's it like working with James Langford? I saw him on TV being interviewed about this movie a month or so ago. He said he was looking forward to it."

Alexandra did a mock shudder. "James Langford. I was warned he'd be a handful before I ever got here, and he's more than lived up to his star billing."

Naomi's eyes widened. "You don't like him?"

Alexandra held up her hand. "Unfortunately we haven't exactly hit it off, or I should say *I* haven't."

Ginger frowned "He looks so nice. Are you guys going to kiss and stuff?"

Alexandra shrugged. "Umm, hmm. It's in the script all right. And there are actual fights between him and me as husband and wife because our characters don't get along either. That's the thrust of the whole thing. There's a lot of physicality in this movie. It's very intense."

Naomi wasn't convinced about the innocence of it all. "You won't have to get hit will you?"

Alexandra laughed. "Nigel Garretson is all for realism so it looks like I might have a few bruises before we're through, but I'm not going to get beat up or anything. The idea is to make it look as real as possible."

All three sat down in the living room, Ginger and Naomi full of questions when the door to the trailer opened and James Langford stuck his head in.

Alexandra tensed. The nerve of that man! "Hi James, what can I do for you?"

Without waiting for an invitation he let himself in and walked into the living room, all smiles. "Word travels fast. I heard there were two more of you, Alexandra, but I had to see it with my own eyes to believe it. Three beautiful women and you're identical. Incredible! So are you all into acting, or just my fiancé here?" he asked with a flick of his head toward Alexandra.

Alexandra's mouth flew open. "Fiancé! Since when am I your fiancé?"

The absolute soul of counterfeit charm, he shrugged his shoulders good-naturedly. "I haven't gotten around to asking you yet, but that's the way I think of you in my heart, Alexandra. You know we're destined to be together, Love. I haven't made any secret of the fact that I worship the ground you walk on."

Alexandra couldn't help but laugh at the drama James created, nonstop. She stole a quick glance at Naomi and Ginger who sat open-mouthed and wide-eyed nearby, clearly star struck at being in the same room with the Hollywood heartthrob. They were blushing!

Alexandra waved away James' impromptu performance, including the part about worshipping the ground she walked on. "Oh that. We'll talk," she said, passing it off in better humour than she was feeling toward him at the moment.

James winked and blew Alexandra a kiss before his attention drifted to Naomi and Ginger. "So if you two ladies are not in the entertainment industry, pray tell what you do?"

Ginger was the first to speak. "I'm a freelance writer and an office manager." She turned to Naomi whose eyes were still glued to James. "And our sister Naomi here is a computer programmer."

James threw his hands in the air. "What a waste, two stunning women who should be before the cameras. It's obvious the camera would fall in love with you both, because it absolutely adores Alexandra. I think I should introduce you to Nigel Garretson, our director. I can't imagine he wouldn't want to use all three of you sometime in the future.

What a picture that would be, and I would want to be cast in it as well. You could all be my paramours. It would be box office gold."

Ginger laughed. "Ahh, sorry, not interested."

Naomi was shaking her head vigourously. "Me either." She glanced over at Ginger. "I don't think either one of us are looking to make any career changes. We both enjoy what we do," to which Ginger quickly nodded her agreement.

He looked haplessly at Alexandra. "I guess that means we only have access to one goddess, and it warms the cockles of my heart to know we have you in cinema heaven."

Alexandra rolled her eyes. "James...."

Now in full flight, he was not to be denied. "Don't scold the little boy with his nose pressed against the candy store windowpane. I can look, can't I? Dream? And excuse me but I have to ask, are either one of you or both of you married?"

Ginger and Naomi both held up their ring hands, speaking as one which was not an unusual occurrence. "Very happily," they said in perfect unison.

James was obviously having the time of his life. "So I haven't fallen through the looking glass, you three are actually triplets."

Alexandra smiled, amused by his over the top performance. The only thing missing was a camera. "Yes, we're triplets, James."

He looked at her reprovingly. "I'd like to know why you never told me."

Alexandra raised her eyebrows. "How about because I didn't consider it to be something you needed to know?"

He wagged his finger at her. "Tsk, tsk, my little one. Let's not be testy."

Alexandra checked her watch, wondering as she did so if perhaps he hadn't tipped a glass despite the early hour. In all fairness though, she'd never smelled it on him during filming. "All right, James. We don't have very long before I have to go to set, so I'd like to spend what time I have left with my sisters. I haven't seen them for almost a year, and I've been looking forward to this visit. Okay?"

He shrugged his shoulders eloquently. "Okay, Alexandra, I can take a hint. I'll see you in a little while." He turned to Naomi and Ginger. "Goodbye ladies, it's been a pleasure."

And with that he made a typically dramatic exit, pausing at the door for one last James Langford megawatt smile. He was a handsome man, and he knew it.

Once they were sure he was out of earshot, Naomi turned to Alexandra. "I saw him in Chicago Morning. He's good in that show. Very sweet."

Ginger was equally as enthusiastic. "And very handsome I might add. I can't imagine you don't like him, Alexandra. I would think he'd be a joy to work with. You're so lucky!"

Alexandra bugged her eyes out. "Lucky! Our personalities don't click at all, although I'm trying to power through that. I don't find him easy to work with on set, but I must say he has gone out of his way to help me when he thought I needed it. But still...."

Naomi's curiosity hadn't even begun to be satisfied. "I think you need to give him a chance. He seems very impressed with you. Why would he call you his fiancé I wonder."

Alexandra waved her hand at what she considered to be a ridiculous notion. "I have no idea why he would say such a thing because it's not true. Even if he were serious I still wouldn't be interested. Not at all."

Ginger studied her sister. "Okay, why?"

Alexandra shrugged. "I'm just not is all. He's not my type."

Naomi flicked a speck of imaginary lint off her navy cotton trousers. "That old biological clock is ticking, sister dear. I've heard you say that about hunk after hunk. Doesn't anyone pique your interest?"

Alexandra smiled. "I'm glad you asked me that. First of all I don't have a heart of stone, I haven't had time to get interested in anyone. Even when they're in the same business as I am. It's either there or it's not. I don't have to tell you that, Naomi. Look at Ritchie. Now he was hot by anyone's standards, but it wasn't there for you."

Naomi raised her hands in surrender. "Okay, I get it. But James Langford...."

Ginger leaned forward. "Have you had any kissing scenes with him yet?"

Alexandra smiled. "A few."

Ginger's mouth formed a perfect o. "All right then, dish! What was it like? Is he a good kisser?"

Alexandra was already shaking her head. "Sorry to burst your bubble, but no. His kisses don't do anything for me but mind you they're movie kisses or supposed to be. He goes for the gold every time, but his lips are cold. Some people might like the way he kisses. There's a whole list of women who've said they do but I'm not one of them."

Naomi pulled a face. "Aren't you supposed to do a love scene with him?"

Ginger was interested. "Love scene? You mean as in bed?"

Alexandra chuckled. "As in bed, naked too I might add."

Naomi and Ginger reacted in unison again. "Naked!"

Alexandra looked resigned. "Naked. I'm dreading it with everything I have in me, but my agent said this was too good a role to turn down since I'm trying to get noticed by the bigwigs in Hollywood. James has even said he wants me to star with him in his next picture."

Ginger was still aghast. "You mean you take off *everything* in front of *everyone*?"

Alexandra gave her a leveling look, amused. "I won't be parading around nude for all the world to see. Besides most sex scenes, at least for the movies that are going to be shown in theatres, are simulated, but yes I'll be in the nude. It will be a closed set, at least that's what I've been told to expect."

Naomi was equally as nonplussed. "There might not be a lot of people, but the camera will show the world what it sees so what's the difference?"

Alexandra looked at her. "Thanks, Naomi. Now I feel much better, thank you."

Ginger was not to be pacified. "Naomi's right. There's no way you can get out of it. Speak to the director and tell him you're not comfortable with it, that you've changed your mind."

Alexandra looked resigned. "It was Nigel's idea, his vision for the film and he discussed it with me before I agreed to do it."

Naomi sighed. "And there's no way out?"

Alexandra smiled sadly. "Not unless I want to be fired or sued for breach of contract. Don't worry about me, I'll get through it and naturally they'll be discreet. I won't be thrown to the wolves."

Ginger was quiet for a moment. "I guess if you have to be naked in front of somebody, it might as well be James Langford."

Naomi winked. "And I suppose he'll also be naked."

Alexandra blushed to the roots of her hair. "Yes, he will."

Ginger laughed. "I can't believe you're actually going to go through with it." She held up her hand to forestall any further justification. "I understand you have to do it and there could be worse things than seeing James Langford naked, but you're a lot braver than I ever would be. And here we always called you the shy one. Little Alexandra isn't shy anymore."

Alexandra laughed. "I'm shy, I'll pretend I'm somewhere else, anywhere else but in bed with James Langford."

Naomi smiled. "You could pretend to be somebody else. Get through it that way."

Alexandra nodded. "Now you're beginning to get the picture. Remember, I'm not Alexandra Martel, am I? I'm Sari Patton, wife of whacko billionaire Hubert Patton. I'll leave Alexandra Martel here in the trailer and come back for her later. It will be Sari who takes her clothes off for her husband, not me. Think of it that way, that's what an actor does. They get into the skin of the character and become them. You leave yourself behind, and come back to being who you really are, later."

Ginger smiled. "So who are we talking to now, Sari Patton or our sister?"

Alexandra pulled a face. "Smart ass."

Ginger held up her hands in mock defense. "Relax! I got it. But you'd better hope Gram doesn't get wind of this nude scene of yours. If I were you I'd keep that little tidbit to myself if you don't want her to go into overdrive. If she even knew about it she'd be up here having a go at the director, the poor man."

Alexandra grinned. "First of all Gram never has to find out if neither of you tell her because *I* certainly don't plan to. And second of all I'd buy tickets to a throw down between Nigel Garretson and Gram, and my money would be on Gram. Nigel has the reputation of a tyrant but don't tell Gram that either or she *will* be up here going at him. I think the least said about what goes on here the better."

Naomi raised her eyebrows. "And you don't think she's going to want to see the movie when it comes out? I think she's watched mostly everything you've been in, so prepare yourself. She likes to see her granddaughter on the screen, I guess she'll be seeing a lot more of her than usual in Retribution."

Alexandra couldn't help but laugh. "Fair enough, but the love scene between James and I is not explicit. So at least that's in my favour where Gram's concerned."

Ginger winked. "You keep telling yourself that, Sis. When she sees it they can do another movie: Gram Unleashed."

Alexandra pulled a face. "Oh, Ginger, you're so funny. My sides are hurting."

Naomi stretched her legs out in front of her. "Okay, got it. Alexandra is making her debut in her birthday suit."

Ginger's mouth fell open. "Something just occurred to me. If people see you nude,

Alexandra, then they've seen Naomi and I naked too because we're all the same. Now isn't *that* a comforting thought."

Alexandra and Naomi had a good chuckle about Ginger's outrage before Naomi held up her hand. "Okay, let's change the subject. According to you, it's a no go for James Langford, but there're plenty of men walking around here. Has anyone else caught your eye by any chance? What about that Beau guy you mentioned to me?"

Alexandra smiled coyly.

Naomi and Ginger were immediately interested. "Dish!" they said in unison.

Alexandra waggled her eyebrows comically. "Okay, you're forcing this out of me, but I met this guy yesterday, quite by accident and I couldn't stop looking at him. I felt that lightning bolt both of you say you felt when you met Shane, Ginger, and the same one you experienced all those years ago with Hayden, Naomi. So who knows? There might be hope for me yet."

Naomi was immediately on fire. "Details, Sis. We want details."

Alexandra sighed, smiling. "It was his eyes that stood out to me the most. They're like pale green, quite unusual. His hair was long, not ponytail long, but down to his collar and combed away from his face and he was clean-shaven. We're all tall and he was taller than me, so I'd say about six foot two or so, and had what you'd call an athletic build. I remember too he had great teeth, nice and white when he smiled. I liked his hands too, rugged looking, like he was used to doing hard work."

Ginger was the first to speak. "It sounds like you got a good look at him, and not much wonder he turned your head. Did you get a name besides Beau?"

Alexandra nodded. "Yep. Beau Remington. Dr. Beau Remington."

Again in unison, Naomi and Ginger: "Doctor!"

Alexandra nodded. "Yes, doctor. He's a veterinarian who'll be on set when they start using the animals. He says he's an emergency and critical care specialist, so he'll be here in case something happens to the dogs. I was quite taken with him."

Naomi was still gawking. "And can we assume he was quite taken with you too?"

Alexandra shrugged. "He seemed to be."

Ginger spread her hands. "Did you make plans to hook up or anything? Like exchange phone numbers? Stuff like that?"

Alexandra shook her head. "Nothing like that. I think it's a case of if we happen to run into each other on set or something."

Ginger was aghast. "That's it? You go all gaga over this guy and then let him walk away?"

Alexandra laughed. "What should have I done, tackled him? Demanded his personal information? If he'd wanted me to have it, he'd have given it to me or asked for mine. He didn't, and you know what that means."

Ginger watched Alexandra intently. "No, what?"

Alexandra gave her sister the *dah* look. "That he's either married or in a committed relationship. That's what that means."

Naomi shook her head with purpose. "That's not what that means at all. He was giving out vibes by the sounds of things."

Alexandra shrugged again. "He was definitely giving out vibes, unless I'm so rusty at this I wasn't picking up on his cues. But then James saw me talking to him and interrupted us. I had to leave, and James went back, so heaven only knows what he said to him. For all I know he might have told him I was his fiancé. I wouldn't put it past him."

Ginger was serious. "You've got to get that straightened out. This James Langford is warning everyone off because he has plans for you. Are you seriously not interested at all in James? It doesn't seem like you are."

Alexandra shook her head adamantly. "Not at all."

Ginger folded her arms. "Then you have to talk to this Beau guy."

Alexandra chuckled. "And say what? Oh by the way, I'm available for the taking, Dr. Remington. I thought you should know that in case you're lonely some night."

Ginger reproved her with a playful glare. "Don't be silly, but when you see him again let him know you're interested is what I'm saying."

Alexandra stared at her, amused. "How would I do that?"

Ginger smiled. "You're the actress. Think of something."

* * *

It was a pleasantly warm evening with a delightful breeze off Belleisle Bay as Beau went about his barn chores. First he'd taken care of the dogs and spent time with them before heading down to work with the horses. They'd have to stay outside for another half hour or so while he cleaned their stalls, put down fresh bedding, replenished their mangers and filled their water buckets.

Young Chance didn't know it yet, but he was going to go for a little ride later, while it was still light. He knew the chestnut was always raring for a good go and so his run was along the old logging road over to the Walkerton Place, abandoned now for years. The fact was it was tied up in an estate and couldn't be sold, so the barns and farmhouse had not only fallen into disrepair but fallen *down* which was a real shame. He'd wanted to buy the property when he was looking for a place a few years ago, but it was not to be had so he'd settled for something a little further along the bay. The price had been a bit higher than he'd been in the market for, but the buildings were in great shape and the house even better. There hadn't been much to do in the way of renovations. Everything had worked out for the best.

So after a quick supper he'd gone back down to the barn and while the other two Chances were already stretched out on their straw, young Chance nickered to him hopefully. He began to paw his stall when he saw Beau get the saddle blanket down.

Later, the young horse danced under him as they approached the logging road. Anxious for his cue to run, when it came he streaked toward the finish line, which was a field about a kilometre up ahead. Blowing hard when they reached it, Chance finally settled down and an hour later they were back home. Only then was the horse satisfied to return to his stall, munching hay as Beau cooled him down. All three horses were on their feet waiting for their nightly grooming and he spent time brushing them and cleaning their hooves.

Back at the house he took a refreshing shower before slipping into a clean T-shirt and a pair of cargo shorts, then stretched out on the verandah with a tall glass of iced tea.

It had been an interesting couple of days, satisfying as they all were when he got to help animals. He thought about poor Barney and indeed Old Ned, although the hermit had gone on to a much better place. Not so for Barney who was unable to fend for himself, chained up as he'd been. Luckily that story had a happy ending. Paulette Nowlan would slowly bring the dog back to a healthy weight and then find a loving home for him.

He thought too about meeting that actress yesterday on the movie set. He'd Googled her, and she was one good-looking woman. It didn't say anything online about her being engaged to anyone, and there were no pictures of her with that actor who claimed to be her fiancé, whatever his name was. He was as overbearing as they came, so he'd give the whole situation a wide path.

The last thing he needed was to get tangled up in someone else's drama.

Nope, stay clear, he thought as he got up and headed indoors. It was time to turn in after a typically busy day, but he'd no sooner climbed into bed when his cellphone rang. It had to be the office because the calls were forwarded. In all probability it was an emergency. Grabbing the phone he glanced at the screen. It wasn't the clinic at all. He gawked at the screen. This had to be some kind of joke. It couldn't be Alexandra Martel calling him!

Chapter 5

Yet that's what it said: incoming call from Alexandra Martel. He answered the call. "Hello?"

"Hi," she said cheerfully.

That was her sultry, well-modulated voice all right. He wouldn't forget how that sounded anytime soon.

"Hi, yourself," he said, completely knocked offside and trying not to sound like it. "Is this the lady I was talking to yesterday on the movie set?"

She chuckled, and even that sounded sexy. "I feel like I should apologize for making this call. I'm kind of old school I guess and it's the first time I've ever done something like this. I Googled you on the spur of the moment and here I am."

She probably never *had* done something like this before. When a woman looked like she did, she'd have to beat the men off, not make the call herself.

"I'm glad you called," he told her as he continued to recover himself. "It's nice to hear from you."

She'd have no idea he was in bed, not that he minded talking to her here, but he somehow didn't want her to know because it might embarrass her. So pulling back the covers slowly he got to his feet and went to sit in the armchair by the window. *I'm on the phone with Alexandra Martel* he thought again in a pinch me if I'm dreaming kind of moment.

"I didn't catch you at a bad time, did I?"

"Oh no," he lied, "I was just kicking back."

Not many people were in bed at nine o'clock at night although from what he'd heard, movie people did tend to keep early hours too. So that might be where *she* was at the moment. He'd never ask such a personal question, not knowing her.

He suddenly remembered James Langford's warning and as reluctant as he was to have this call end, he knew it was only right to address what could be the elephant in the room. "Miss Martel...."

"Call me Alexandra, please," she said.

"Okay then, Alexandra, the actor you're starring with in the movie...."

"James Langford?"

"That's his name. Anyway, he basically warned me away from you yesterday. He told me you were his fiancé and so I have to be honest, I don't want to get mixed up in the middle of someone else's business."

She chuckled again and he liked the sound of it. It made him feel happy, light. "Don't pay any attention to him. He's been telling people he and I are engaged, and I can't for the life of me understand why he'd do that. I only heard about it myself this morning, so it doesn't mean anything. There is no truth to it."

"And if he does ask you to marry him?"

"The answer would be no. I have no interest in Mr. Langford other than on a professional basis. There could never be anything more than that between him and me."

He could feel relief surge through him like quicksilver. If ever he had connected with a woman it'd been yesterday when Alexandra Martel had walked into his life, and he would love nothing better than to get to know her. The problem was, he had no clue how that would ever happen under the present circumstances. If something were to come from any of this, it promised to be complicated.

"That's good," he said, wearing a broad smile, "because I'd like to...."

Just then all three dogs erupted into a cacophony of barking, racing for the back door as someone started knocking.

"Ooops, sorry about the noise level, Alexandra. There's someone at the door and what you hear is my welcoming committee, or alarm, whichever the situation calls for. Give me a minute."

The dogs fell silent on command, their tails wagging in unison as he opened the door and there stood Dr. Jen holding a bottle of white wine. He remembered he was clad only in boxer briefs at the same time she noticed the same thing. It would be a toss up as to whose face was redder.

"Ahh, give me a minute, Jen," he told his colleague. "I'm talking on the phone."

Dr. Jen stepped inside, averting her eyes. "That's okay, Beau. No worries. I'm a little later than I intended to be."

One thing he liked about Jen, professionally speaking, was her clear distinct voice. It was a tremendous asset, especially when they were masked in surgery. No whispery voice for Jen, and unfortunately it carried loud and clear over the sound waves where he was sure

Alexandra heard what was said with superb clarity. Great!

Beau still had the phone to his ear when Alexandra spoke. "Oh my goodness, this was a bad idea. I'm sorry. Gotta go!" and with that she was gone before he could say anything to stop her.

"No! Wait!" he yelled anyway as he made his way back into the bedroom although he knew she was no longer on the line. And the likelihood of seeing her on set again and be given a chance to explain, was slim at best. He'd bet good money she'd block him as soon as she ended the call. Perfect!

Trying to resign himself to the lost opportunity, he set the phone down on the night table and hauled on jeans and a T-shirt before returning to the living room barefoot. Jen had taken up residence in the same armchair he'd vacated moments ago, her feet tucked comfortably up under her.

Forcing a smile he plunked down in his recliner. "What brings you here, Jen? Did I forget you were coming?"

Sometimes things did genuinely slip his mind, even though he figured he wouldn't forget he had a date. This felt more like a booty call. He had to get what could turn out to be an embarrassing situation straightened out before it went any further. The last thing he wanted to do was insult her and therefore possibly lose her from the clinic. Now that would be a true loss.

Dr. Jen was a sturdily built girl who might even be called pretty if she did something with her hair other than scrape it back into that no-nonsense ponytail. But it wouldn't matter anyway he thought because he valued her as a colleague and that was all. He got that she might be lonely, what with her moving to this quiet community from Toronto, but she'd been determined to fulfill her dream to be a small town vet. She could have done that nicely in Ontario, but to make things even more interesting she had closed her eyes and turned in a circle three times before placing a forefinger on a map of Canada. The winner had been the tiny settlement of Hatfield Point, Kings County, New Brunswick.

She seemed happy enough with her choice of location and had told him more than once she was living her dream. He was glad she was settling in so well, but he had to make it plain without offending her that he was not part of it.

Jen was beaming as she looked around the room, as though she was having her very *own* pinch me moment. "You didn't forget, Beau. I thought I'd drop by and say hello, share a little vino, discuss our schedule for tomorrow. You know, kind of hang out for a while."

He forced himself to relax, at least be polite. Would it hurt to have a glass of wine since she was kind enough to bring it with her? The truth was he didn't care for wine, but she obviously did if she'd gone to all the trouble to buy a bottle of something she'd thought he'd like to share with her. He knew it was quite a drive to find a store that sold it around here. And again, he didn't want to offend her but by the same token he didn't believe in pussyfooting around either. There was some stuff that had to get said.

He shifted uncomfortably. "Jen, the last thing I want to do is hurt your feelings. I respect you. I like you, but only as a friend."

She reddened. "Okay, I guess this was a bad idea coming here tonight."

"I don't want you to feel you can't come here, but I have to be upfront with you. I don't think of you as anything more than a colleague, a friend. I don't see anything romantic happening between the two of us."

"Did I ever tell you the story of my mother and father?"

Now that surprised him. "I don't believe I ever heard you mention them."

She smiled and it brought her otherwise plain features to life. "They were both veterinarians, that's where I got the idea to be one too. You know, keep the family tradition going. Anyway, my father had this little practice about the same size we have here. He ran it alone for a few years and then along came my mother. Female veterinarians weren't as common in those days as they are now, but she got hired by my father and, well, do I need to connect the dots? They fell in love and had me."

He nodded thoughtfully. "That's a great story. But you can't think that just because...."

She laughed merrily, clearly enjoying herself. She was pleasant enough to work with, and all business. He was seeing a different side of her tonight, but he still did not want anything from her other than a friendly, professional relationship, agreeable personality or not.

She leaned forward. "Don't you see?"

He looked at her, perplexed. "See what?"

"I've told you the story of how I happened to come here to New Brunswick. Remember?"

He nodded slowly. "I remember you telling me how that went."

"I put my finger on the map, ready to go wherever it landed, whether it was Nunavut or Victoria. It happened to be Hatfield Point, on Belleisle Bay. You don't think it's odd I chose this place, found a veterinary practice here run by a single doctor, and when I contacted you, you happened to be looking to hire another vet? Hello! You and I were meant to be together. Think about it! It's as plain as the nose on your face."

"Jen...."

"All of that doesn't sound the tiniest bit serendipitous to you?"

He was even more uncomfortable now. "I think there are coincidences, yes, but that's all. I wasn't sitting in my office down there, lonely, hoping a female veterinarian would cross my path. I know several female veterinarians, some of which are available, and all of whom I'm friendly with, but not intimate."

"But don't you see?"

He was tired, and this game was starting to get on his nerves. If the cork weren't still in the bottle he'd suspect she'd already sampled the product. Okay, he'd play along for another few minutes but then she was going to leave, good working relationship at stake or not.

"Don't I see what?"

Her eyes sparkled. She was loving this. Had she been biding her time to make her move? Incredible!

"My father wasn't sitting there all lonely waiting for a female veterinarian to come along either, because he didn't realize how much he wanted a relationship until it started to happen. How come I'm the only one here who can see the parallels between the two situations?"

He had to chuckle. It was strange he had to admit, but he'd hazard a guess Dr. Jen spent more than a little of her spare time surfing serendipity sites online. She seemed very familiar with the whole concept. Okay so he was a Pisces. He'd bet if he asked her about what was ahead for his zodiac sign she'd know it to the letter, as well as her own. One thing was for sure, she was on fire tonight. He didn't see himself hitting the sheets anytime soon, alone, at least until this thing was properly hashed out.

She was surprising him. He hadn't expected her to come at him from this direction, but you never knew what someone was thinking.

"I can see the similarities, but that's all they are, Jen, similarities. You're not awakening any long dormant loneliness or anything. I'm fine with my life the way it is."

"But you're handsome, and you're all alone."

He had to smile as he looked around the room, Ajax, Carley and Ron all snoozing peacefully beside the empty fireplace. "As you can see I'm hardly alone. I have all the company I need at the moment with these three, and there's also three horses in the barn."

She was still beaming. "Why are men so stubborn?" she asked no one in particular, although he felt he should answer.

He settled back deeper into the recliner. "I didn't know we were."

"I'll tell you then, you are so stubborn it's infuriating."

"And if I wasn't being so infuriatingly stubborn, as you put it, what would I be doing?"

She laughed. "You'd be understanding that you and I are meant to be together, at least letting it flow instead of doing everything in your power to shut us down before we've even had a chance."

He leaned forward again, his elbows on his knees. "That's what I'm trying to say to you, Jen. I don't see that with us. You're a great girl, it's just that...."

She pulled a face. "Is that what you see when you look at me? A girl? Well look again," and with that she pulled the long-sleeved pullover over her head revealing a fitted tank underneath with an abundance of cleavage struggling for release. Next went the running pants and under those were fitted bike shorts that hugged ample womanly curves. As a finishing touch she reached back and pulled her ponytail free of the scrunchie and a cascade of soft brown curls tumbled around her shoulders. Dr. Jennifer Tuttle was transformed before his very eyes. The change was astonishing, and he was aware he was staring, and not just at her twinkling green eyes. She was obviously one of those people whose eye colour changed with their mood. He'd seen that before but not quite as dramatic as this.

Her smile was coquettish, which he would have sworn was completely out of character for her, but there it was in full bloom. It was the kind of smile a woman wore when she knew she'd finally gotten the attention she wanted from a certain someone. In this case it was him, and she'd accomplished it if for no other reason than because of how different she looked.

"Dr. Jen, you've been hiding a lot under that uniform of yours. I'll give you that."

"So?"

"So, what? You're beautiful, okay? I never saw such a transformation and you didn't even need to put on any makeup."

He was instantly reminded of someone else who didn't need cosmetics, although she was wearing makeup when they'd met. Still, he'd bet most women would have had to have a lot more slathered on to help the camera fall in love with them. Alexandra Martel was not one of those women. Whomever the makeup artist was, they deserved an award for merely highlighting her natural beauty, not burying it under layers of greasepaint.

Jen was aglow. "I'm glad you're seeing me in a different light. I would say mission accomplished if you're finally taking notice of me. Told ya so." she taunted him good-naturedly.

He grinned. "Busted. Now tell me if you came here tonight hoping you'd find me in bed. I'm sure I told you I turn in early. You did, didn't you?"

She blushed again. This time the heightened colour was most becoming because it extended all the way from her face to her plunging neckline. "Okay, I'm busted. You know, Beau, I recall reading once how some people don't fall in love until they've been, umm, intimate. It awakens something in the brain."

He had to laugh outright at that one. "I think you made that one up, Dr. Jen, because that's a lot of hooey."

"No, seriously, it has to do with compatibility."

"I think that's decided long before you climb under the covers. And no, we're not going to sleep together so get that out of your mind. Sorry to mess up what seems to be very carefully laid plans, excuse the pun, but you're dead wrong on that score. I don't usually sleep with my friends, or colleagues for that matter. You've laid it on thick enough here tonight but I'm hoping we can set all this aside and remain friends."

She was crestfallen and he regretted he'd had to dash her dreams. It wasn't something he'd never experienced himself. He had, with Patty Mooreville in high school. He'd been besotted with the cute blonde, had a terminal case of puppy love. He well remembered the agony of working up the courage to ask her to the tenth grade school dance, and her heartless rejection of him. He'd been a late bloomer and she had laughed when he asked her out, like it was the most ridiculous thing she'd ever heard. His heart had been broken for sure, but when he saw her from time to time now he thanked his lucky stars she hadn't said yes if today was the future he'd have been looking forward to back then. Turns out she'd peaked early, had already gone through two husbands and was chain-smoking her way to a third divorce. No thanks.

She shook her head, and he surely hoped those weren't tears gathering in her eyes. Thankfully it was eyestrain because a moment later she was laughing again. "Okay, Dr. Beau, fair enough, but so you know, I'm not going to stop trying. Or should I say stop hoping because I've never been one to make a nuisance of myself. I'm going to keep manifesting you until it becomes real. Our relationship will come to pass because that's what I'm asking the universe for. I have to have patience is all."

How could anyone not like Dr. Jen? She had enough spunk and good cheer for two women and would make a wonderful partner for some man some day. In that moment, just fleetingly, he wished it could be him, and then it was gone. His kneejerk reaction to things had never been wrong, and it wasn't now.

She slipped her pullover back into place and pulled her hair into the scrunchie, visibly relaxing when everything was returned to its normal place, well except for her outer exercise pants. She folded those up and put them in her purse, opting to go with the bike shorts.

"You know what, Beau?" she asked in her usual laidback manner.

"What?"

"I'm not going to apologize for coming here tonight and laying everything on the table. I'm proud of myself for having the gumption to take the bull by the horns. I've always liked that about myself."

He had to chuckle. "I'm glad you did too. It's good we can be upfront with each other."

If anyone could take an awkward situation and turn it around, it was Jen, her good nature contagious. Some lucky man would win her heart someday.

She looked at him with a gleam in her eye. "You know, Beau, I spent good money on that bottle of wine. Can't we at least have a drink together, sort of a toast to what will be in the future?"

"You're an optimist, I'll give you that, but I'm not into wine. Don't care for the taste of it myself."

"Do you have any apple juice, or Ginger ale by any chance?"

His nice long sleep was getting further and further away because it seemed the irrepressible Jennifer Tuttle wasn't in a mood to leave any time soon. One good thing though, he believed her when she said she wouldn't make a nuisance of herself. If what he knew about her so far meant she'd merely hold onto the hope that someday things would be different, and not get in his face about it, then fine. If it were any other way they'd be in trouble because that kind of tension could quickly ruin a working relationship.

"I have some apple juice, why? You think adding that to wine will work?"

"Where did you do your partying? Add apple juice and some club soda and you have a white wine apple spritzer."

"First of all I wasn't much of a partier, and second of all it doesn't sound like a guy's drink. But because you're being such a good sport about all of this I don't think it'll hurt me to have one white wine apple spritzer. Then it's back home with you and you can take the rest of it with you. Deal?"

"Deal," she said, reaching for the bottle. "Now you can do the honour of popping the cork and I'll try to find us some glasses. I don't suppose you have wine glasses."

"No, no wine glasses. There are some water glasses in the cupboard by the sink. Those will have to do. And the apple juice is in the fridge. I'll have to imagine what it would taste like with Ginger ale because I don't have any of that stuff in the house."

"I'll pour," she announced when Beau had uncorked the bottle and left it with her in the kitchen.

She came in moments later with two full tumblers.

"Whoa there, Nellie! You must have used the entire bottle. I don't want all of that and you're certainly not going to drink it then get back on the road."

"I think it's too late for that anyway because I helped myself to some while I was in the kitchen. I can't remember the last time I had a drink and I'm already feeling tipsy. I don't think I'd better drive at all."

Great! He was now a top candidate for dunce of the year award. She might have backed off when he suggested she do so, but the little minx had kept to her original agenda all along. He sighed in exasperation and before he could reach ahead for the glasses she had already gulped own half of hers. His opinion of her took a one hundred and eighty degree turn and immediately headed the other way. He would have thought better of her, but this seemed like one last trick up her sleeve.

He knew what it felt like to have unrequited feelings for someone, and not just sweet Patty from high school. He'd been in a couple of serious relationships, one that he'd ended himself. In the other he'd been dumped. He had to have patience with Jen until she worked this thing out. One thing was certain, they were going to have a very long serious discussion tomorrow and whether she stayed or left, the matter would be dealt with. He hated the thought of losing her talent and skill as a veterinarian, but this would go no further than what was turning out to be the unavoidable tonight.

"Come on, Jen. You're going to be sick all over the place," he said reprovingly as he took both glasses from her and carried them back to the kitchen. "This is not cool at all."

"I'm sorry," she said, her face puckering.

"Don't you dare start crying," he warned her, still trying to keep it light and stop this thing from escalating any further.

"I'm not going to do that," she said, obviously working to keep her emotions, or more to the point the sting of his rejection, in check. "I never do the weepy female thing, you know that. I'm a strong woman."

"You are," he agreed, "but tears are not a sign of weakness."

"There you go," she giggled. "That's what I would call a Beau-ism. You're a very smart man."

He could tell by how hard the wine was hitting her she wasn't a drinker, so he'd indulge her this one faux pas, until tomorrow.

Young Carley trotted over to him and licked his hand, which meant she had to answer the call of nature. Going to the back door he let her out and watched as she sniffed the ground then headed for the far end of the enclosure. She proceeded to water a shrub before scratching vigourously. Blades of grass flew as she finished her routine and trotted back to the house and in past Beau.

He locked the door for the night since Jen would be his overnight guest, in the spare bedroom, and headed back into the living room. There was no Jen. It didn't take a genius to find her, because she was under the covers in *his* bed already asleep or pretending to be. Either way he was headed in the other direction to bunk down in the spare bedroom himself. Oh, were they ever going to have a talk tomorrow!

Glancing back he went to retrieve his cellphone from the table and turn out the light, but not before he noticed her clothes, all of them, on the floor beside his bed. Oh, Dr. Jen.

Chapter 6

For the life of her Alexandra could not get to sleep. She kept replaying her mortification over and over in her mind. Not many would guess that an actress who made herself vulnerable for a living, was actually very shy. She had never in her life called a man the way she'd done with Beau tonight. Sure, a longstanding male friend, but never a man she'd just met and was interested in getting to know. Most women wouldn't think twice about it, not in this day and age and perhaps that's the way it should be. Still....

The call had been a short one and he did seem pleased to hear from her, or was she imagining it? He *had* asked about her involvement with James Langford. But then she'd heard the knocking on his door, him going to answer it: "Ahhh, give me a minute, Jen. I'm talking on the phone." And then *Jen* had come through loud and clear: "That's okay, Beau. No worries. I'm a little later than I intended to be." He obviously had a girlfriend, or a wife, even if he didn't wear a ring.

Whatever his arrangement was, this is where she, Alexandra, bowed out. She turned off her phone, which was a bad idea should anyone be trying to reach her in case of an emergency. After an hour or so she'd turned the thing back on and vowed she'd never call a man again and make a fool of herself. Once was enough, no make that twice because she remembered Naomi and Ginger daring her to call Toby Moorehouse and ask him to the junior prom. Naomi and Ginger both had dates, and she was the odd person out so taking the dare she'd made the call. And low and behold even the least popular boy in the class already had a date, a new girlfriend she'd not heard about. To make matters worse, said girlfriend had gotten on the phone to defend her prize. This felt the same.

She could never forget the humiliation of missing her junior prom, and it had been the hardest thing in the world to go back to school after that embarrassment. It had felt like the worst kind of rejection, and she swore she'd never do anything like that again. But she had and it had gone exactly the same way. She was not going to strike out a third time. No way.

* * *

It was almost nine o'clock in the morning by the time Jen stirred and by that time Beau had been up for hours. He'd

115

already turned the horses out and cleaned the barn, fed the dogs and settled them down for the day. He'd looked in on his unexpected guest once or twice to make sure everything was all right, and outside of some quite unladylike snoring, she was fine. He could imagine how embarrassed she'd be to face him this morning. That might account in part for the delay, but last night's wine had set her back on her heels. He was arranging some fresh bacon in the frying pan ahead of the eggs when she put in an appearance.

"Well, finally," he winked at her when he turned to face her in the kitchen. "I thought you were going to sleep around the clock."

She shook her head gently, he noticed, looking a little green around the gills. "I guess I was more tired than I realized," she said, her eyes not meeting his.

"I'm cooking breakfast, fresh bacon and eggs. How hungry are you?"

"No breakfast for me, Beau. My stomach's a little upset."

"I got the impression last night you were quite the partier in university, but it doesn't seem so does it?"

She shook her head for the second time, and he thought about her headache as she did so. In all likelihood she had a doozy if her pained expression was anything to go by.

"All talk, Beau. That's what it was. Wishful thinking. I was the one cracking the books instead of corks. I think I made a fool of myself last night if what I remember is true. I came onto you?"

"You came onto me pretty good," he chuckled.

She looked up at him miserably. "Please tell me that wasn't your bed I woke up in this morning."

He chuckled again. "I hate to rub salt in the wound but yes that was my bed. I slept in the spare bedroom, so no worries."

"We didn't sleep together did we?"

"We did not. Like I said I bunked down in the spare room."

She lowered her face into her hands. "I am so sorry, Beau. I did make a fool of myself, but I hope you don't think it necessary to fire me over this. You are the boss after all. The thought of me ruining our great professional relationship makes me feel even worse than I already do from the wine. My behavior was inexcusable, and I *am* sorry."

He covered the fry pan while the bacon sizzled, taking the nearest seat at the table and indicating with a hand gesture she should sit down across from him. She did so, eyes downcast and he felt sorry for her. Who didn't mess up from time to time.

She raised her eyes. "Beau, I can't say enough how sorry I am I did what I did. I'm not in the habit of throwing myself at men. I can't imagine what you must think of me."

He studied her for a moment. "How did you come to do it? I thought everything was cool between you and me and then in swept Hurricane Jennifer, someone I'd never met before."

She sighed, resting her elbows on the table and her head on her hands. "I don't know. I guess it's no secret now I've developed feelings for you, Beau, and I went about it all wrong to try to show you how I feel. I know this doesn't sound like an intelligent response, but I do believe in destiny. I was told...."

"Jen! Don't tell me you went to a fortune teller!"

"I don't want to talk about it."

"You did, didn't you! What did he or she tell you?"

"Okay I did, and you won't believe how accurate she was. She even got the first initials of your name right, and that we were both animal doctors. It was uncanny what she knew."

"And I imagine you were filling in the blanks for her as she went along. Sounds like a phony to me."

Her eyes were imploring so he decided to cut her some slack. "All right, she was a true psychic. What did she tell you about me?"

"That you were the one, and all you needed was a little coaxing. She said I'd have to take the bull by the horns and well you know the rest."

He sighed, folding his arms across his chest as he leaned back in the chair. Jen was a top-notch veterinarian and wondered how long she'd be content to stay where she was before wanting to move on to bigger opportunities. But at the end of the day she was only twenty-four years old and like a lot of young people her age, still wet behind the ears when it came to love. He was surprised to hear she would give the time of day to a fortuneteller, but who knew? To each their own, but he wouldn't be roped into any of it. He was not at the whim of the stars and a cup full of tealeaves.

He looked at her meaningfully. "Fortuneteller or no fortuneteller, I don't have to explain how badly this went do I?"

She had to chuckle despite herself. "No, but I hope you're not going to hold it over my head."

"Not at all, but I want you to understand it's not going to happen between you and me."

She was silent for a moment, fidgeting with the salt and peppershakers he'd already set on the table. "I'm not trying to belabour the point, I'm not, but does it help you to know my father felt exactly the same way about my mother at first?"

He'd have to give her an "A" for persistence. "No, it doesn't, so let's leave it right there. I think we have a very good working relationship and that's the way I want to keep it. I want to make my feelings very clear. There's not going to be any foolishness about me coming to my senses. I already have full control of my senses and I don't see us as a couple, ever. It's not there for me, Jen."

She nodded. "That's difficult for me to accept because I'll be very honest with you. I've had a crush on you for a long time, almost from the very beginning."

"You've certainly kept it to yourself and that's what I want you to continue to do. As coldhearted as that sounds, that's the way it has to be I'm afraid if we're going to work together. I can't be walking on eggshells around you all the time. I won't do it."

"I hear you, but it's not going to be easy. So can we still be friends, like before?"

"I don't see why not, but no unannounced visits or should I say uninvited. Last night is not going to happen again, all right? I mean it, Jen."

"You don't have to worry about that, I'm so embarrassed. I know I'm repeating myself but all I can do is say I'm sorry and it *will* never happen again. I promise."

"Good," he said going to the stove to turn the bacon. "I believe you. Now let's put all that behind us. Are you sure you wouldn't like to stay and have breakfast with me?"

Her colouring was still off. "No, I'm going to pass on that but thank you anyway. I think I'm going to be on my way. I'll see you at the office. I don't have anything scheduled for early this morning so I'll be an hour or so later coming in if that's all right with you."

"Take your time."

* * *

Alexandra didn't see how she could get through the day on three hours sleep, her usual good sleeping habits having flown right out the window last night. Her practically sleepless night would show on her face like a neon sign. She'd give the makeup people a run for their money trying to cover her dark circles, and she knew before even putting a toe on set the director

121

was going to have something to say about it. There were plenty of close-ups today not to mention that dreaded kissing scene with James. It was not going to be an easy day.

To be sure, Nigel gave her a second look when she walked in for rehearsal. The slight narrowing of his eyes meant he was in one of his quarrelsome moods and ready to pounce. But after all, she reasoned, he was a perfectionist. It was a feather in her cap she'd been chosen to star alongside James Langford in a Nigel Garretson film, and she'd enjoy the end result. She'd focus on that.

Finally they were ready to start shooting, the dialogue preceding the great reluctant lip lock. As the storyline went, Hubert Patton, James Langford's character, had a mercurial disposition much like the director himself she thought. He could be sweet as pie one moment and then fly off the handle the next. James played his part to perfection, even in rehearsal.

"And Action!" the director called, the camera assistant clicking the slate as the clapperboard is known.

James, as Hubert, was smiling as he sat down on the sofa beside his movie wife, Sari, being played by Alexandra. "My darling, why are you being so tiresome? I would think me taking you back after the way you ran off would mean something to you, humble you perhaps. But no, you're still the grand dame of the house. Let me remind you of something. You're not the one in charge around here, I am. Everything you have came from me and in case you haven't figured it out yet, it has a price tag. You were a starving nobody when we met."

She gave her movie husband one of her practiced condescending looks. "My dear, it's you who would be nothing without me. I am your muse, your inspiration. You don't want to admit that, but we both know it's the truth. I've always believed...."

"Cut!" the director screamed. "Alexandra, I don't want you sitting when you deliver those lines. A haughty contemptuous woman would be on her feet looking down her nose on whomever she was addressing in that fashion."

She looked at the director, surprised. "Oh, sorry. I thought that was the way we rehearsed it."

Fire flew from Nigel's eyes as though she had somehow thrown down the gauntlet. Any excuse for a tantrum. "I beg your pardon. You think you know more about how this scene should be played than I do?"

Alexandra was nonplussed, embarrassed he was shouting at her in front of the crew. The way she'd played it was the way they had rehearsed the scene. Nigel had explained it would put the two characters on a level playing field, not one seeming to have the advantage over the other. James knew it too, but he wouldn't speak up. No, he'd sit there and enjoy seeing her put in her place.

"I don't think I know more than you, Mr. Garretson. I thought I was doing it the way you wanted it. I'm sorry."

He took several steps toward her, clearly fuming. "I am the director!" he shouted. "If I say change it a hundred times from the way we rehearsed it, you change it a hundred times. Do you understand?"

Alexandra could feel eyes burning into her. It had to be her lack of sleep that was making her edgy because the director always had the last say. What had ever possessed her to speak up to him like that? He was so touchy it wouldn't take much to set him off, and it obviously hadn't.

"I understand," she said, her chin up.

In no way would she be cowed, but she had no right to question him. And if he was calling her on it in front of cast and crew, hadn't she essentially put him on the spot in front of everyone? He had to assert his authority.

Nigel glanced around him, his colour still high. "Great, everyone! She understands, so let us do the scene again, people. That is if her majesty is prepared to take direction."

Alexandra smiled, getting to her feet ready to do her best imperious, condescending stare down at James.

"And Action!"

Hands on hips, she repeated her lines.

"Cut!"

She stared at the director. *Now* what had she done wrong? This was a very straightforward scene, there were many that were more complex, but it seemed to her the battle lines had been drawn. She knew he was targeting her so she braced herself for the fallout. She didn't have long to wait.

Nigel stared at her, nostrils flared. "Why are your hands on your hips like that? You look like a spider about to pounce, and I want you to try it sitting down this time. I think we'll do it that way, otherwise you're a little too threatening. You're tall so that's intimidating enough. Let's try it again, and Alexandra, remember, you're put out with your husband, you're not going to attack him."

He pulled his eyes away from her slowly as though reluctant to let her off the hook. "Okay, places everyone. And Action!"

Alexandra lounged against the sofa cushions, one arm stretched out along the back, one hand lying loosely in her lap as she delivered her lines. And then her mind went blank, again. She desperately tried to remember what came next, but nothing. All she heard like a death knell in her ear was "Cut!"

Nigel yelled it so loudly he'd likely damaged his larynx. He then raised the clipboard he was holding and drove it across the room, narrowly missing a camera operator. Members of the crew wisely scurried a safe distance away as the director went into one of his full-blown meltdowns. He kicked a chair across the set while bellowing epithets that would make anyone not used to hearing such gutter talk, blush. It seemed Nigel Garretson had quite a repertoire of curse words and worst of all they were directed squarely at her, even as he swung his attention around the room.

This was without a doubt the worst experience of her career. She'd never in all her years of acting ever blown one single line, and today she'd messed up over and over again. She'd be lucky if she weren't fired. An actor who wasn't prepared, did not know their lines, was a liability. Oh everyone flubbed a line now and again and some actors truly did have trouble memorizing. In her experience the director understood and worked it out. *She'd* never experienced forgetting her lines, until today. Nigel *was* intimidating. Him making a big production of things was only making it worse.

Nigel stood a few feet away, actually panting while Alexandra waited, knowing she was about to feel the full wrath of Nigel Garretson.

It appeared he was trying to get control of himself. When he finally turned in her direction again it did seem as though he was a little less purple. Throughout the entire explosion James reclined on the sofa seeming to know he was immune from it all.

"Miss Martel," Nigel said at length. "You are wasting my time today. You are wasting everyone's time today. So unless you get your act together, quickly, that would make you a complete waste of time. As you are well aware, in the movie industry time is money and I will NOT suffer some little ninny of an actress who cannot bother to take the time to learn her lines. You come to the set looking like you had a hard night. That's not lost on me, young lady, he continued when he saw Alexandra blush guiltily. You may think you are above all of this, have achieved stardom, but it is my job to remind you that you have not, far from it.

"Have you never heard of active experiencing? It is your job to become Sari Patton not Alexandra Martel pretending to be her. You are to make us believe, with my help as your director, that you are that troubled woman hopelessly trapped in a perilous relationship. What I'm getting from you is something you could have phoned in. Today you are a cardboard caricature of Sari Patton and of no use to this movie. If this were a live performance you would be booed off the stage."

He was still breathing hard as he continued. "My team believed you would be an asset to Retribution but let me remind you of one very salient fact. You can be fired and replaced at any given time. I don't like to think I have made a mistake in choosing you for this project, but if I have, so be it. Now, I want you to leave this set, go off alone for a few minutes, collect yourself and when you return, be ready to bring it. And don't bother to shed any tears and ruin my close-ups. I will get this scene from you if it kills me, even if we have to stay here all night. And then, as you know, we have an even more demanding scene waiting after that. I promise you, I will get both of them by the end of shooting tonight. So if you don't want the entire cast and crew to suffer because of your ineptitude, get it together. Now!"

Alexandra did as he suggested and even though she felt like having a good old-fashioned cry, she fought her tears and walked off by herself to collect her thoughts. It was true, she was exhausted, and it showed in the quality of her performance today. Add the capricious Nigel Garretson to the mix and it spelled disaster. One thing was for certain, she would get the sleep she needed tonight and that would start as soon as she got back to her trailer. She would allow no interruptions. If someone wanted in, they'd have to knock down the door. She would also shut off her cellphone.

Today had been embarrassing and it must not be repeated. If she wanted to go anywhere in this industry she had to suck it up, give the director what he wanted no matter how impossible he made things for her. She had worked too hard and too long to fritter it all away because she'd lost a little sleep.

"Feeling, better?" James asked her when she walked back onto the set.

She resisted the urge to glare at him. She'd seen the look on his face when the director was letting her have it. She realized in that moment she disliked him as intensely as she disliked Nigel. They were neck in neck, and in her opinion it wasn't a race anybody would want to win.

"I'm fine," she answered tightly.

"Can I give you a word of advice, Alexandra?"

"No, you may not," she said to him in undertones. "I can get along very well without your advice. But thank you anyway," she thought to add in an attempt to at least keep things civil.

He shrugged. "Have it your way, but if you ask me you could use all the advice you can get because I haven't seen Nigel this pissed off since...."

"Since the last time he was pissed off," she added wickedly. "Skip the lecture, James. I seem to recall you missed a line or two yesterday. I also noted Nigel didn't freak out over it. It pays to have friends in high places I guess, but don't worry about me. I can look after myself, I'm a big girl."

"You didn't go off bawling, so that's a plus. You might like to know I'm impressed, and I don't impress easily."

"I couldn't care less if you're impressed or not," she told him, keeping her voice low.

What she had to say to James was not the business of the crew.

James on the other hand loved the sound of his own voice and assumed everyone else did too. "Suite yourself, it's your career," he said with a Cheshire cat smile, catching the eye of the production assistant who was making it as plain as possible she was one of his devoted fans.

Alexandra only hoped he wouldn't get the PA's trailer mixed up with hers tonight and end up with his unwanted company. Let the production assistant have him and good riddance.

Nigel still hadn't gotten over his snit, but he could find no fault with her as she took his directorial style in stride and did not miss even one line for the rest of the day. Not that they got it on the first take, but the retakes were not her fault. Finally the director was satisfied, and it went to print.

* * *

The man woke up, cramped from sleeping in his SUV. His finances were in a dreadful state, but he had enough space on his card to keep his room for a few more nights if need be. He hadn't been able to find any suitable accommodations in this backwater. He'd had to drive all the way back and forth from Franklin to Belleisle. He remembered when he'd first arrived in the city. He'd waited for hours at the airport for that late flight to arrive two weeks ago, finally catching a glimpse of Alexandra as she was walking through the terminal. The tall good-looking man at her side he recognized as James Langford. Oh he'd done his homework all right. They wore ball caps and sunglasses, which to him were ridiculously inadequate. He knew their size and height, so it wasn't hard to put it all together. She was so close, but it was not the right time to make his move.

It was turning into quite a feat to hang around a small place like Belleisle and not stand out. Everyone knew everyone else. He was lucky this was tourist season, a time when absentee landowners made their trek north to Canadian cottages. So he'd been able to pass himself off as one of those visiting Americans. He'd made a few passes by the movie site, too many if he didn't want to attract attention. He'd have to be more careful. If he could afford to he'd switch vehicles, have a better disguise. But the fact was time was running out for him and if he were going to take her, he'd have to do it soon. All sites dedicated to the movie shoot were well guarded, so it didn't take a genius to figure out she would be too, maybe better.

He had to think harder, be smarter than any of those movie people on any given day, in order to prevail. He almost had everything down to a science now anyway as to how he was going to put it all together. It was only a matter of waiting now, being patient. Sooner or later he'd find her in a vulnerable position and when he did he'd have to act fast.

Chapter 7

Dr. Jen was understandably subdued at the clinic that morning, but Beau understood why she wasn't feeling her best. She'd foolishly chugged a good part of that bottle while pouring their drinks in the kitchen, and then downed more in the living room. He suspected she'd taken what she felt she needed for courage to act completely out of character, otherwise he would never have seen that side of her.

In the hours since the impromptu seduction of her boss she'd had plenty of time to regret her actions, both physically and emotionally, and he was sure she was doing just that. He liked her, she had good energy about her. When she made a mistake, and she'd made a doozy, she was strong enough to face up to it and move on. So would he. He had no intention of ever mentioning it again.

He was busy at his computer when Jen poked her head in later that morning. "I need to talk to you, Beau," she said, already slipping into the chair on the other side of his desk. "We've had a request I want to run by you. A Mrs. Margaret Ratchett called to tell us her cat had a batch of kittens, and the babies are now eight weeks old, and weaned. But this is the part that's upsetting. She wants all of the kittens euthanized."

His eyes widened. "Are they sick?"

"No, they're all healthy according to Mrs. Ratchett. She told Hailey she wanted to enjoy them for a while but had no plans to keep any of them."

"Is that right! Well right out of the gate I have no intention of allowing healthy animals to be euthanized, there are always other options. Has she tried to find homes for the little guys?"

"She says she's tried but hasn't had any luck and can't afford to keep feeding them. It's good I suppose she called here instead of taking matters into her own hands."

"That's right, but why wouldn't she contact the SPCA and see if she could get some help there? They might be overrun with kittens at this time of year, but you never know."

Dr. Jen tightened the scrunchie on her ponytail. "Hailey suggested that too, but she doesn't want to deal with the SPCA for some reason. She was adamant about that."

"Why is that, I wonder. She doesn't know I sit on the board of the local SPCA, and Mrs. Ratchett just got on our radar."

"Hailey also suggested she get the mother cat spayed."

"And what did she say to that?"

"She said she couldn't afford it. She said if she got one female spayed she'd have to get the others fixed too and it would cost too much."

Beau swore under his breath. Mrs. Ratchett was going to get a visit all right.

"But she can afford to have what I assume are healthy animals, euthanized. How many kittens did you say there were, Jen?"

"Five, all calicos."

"Which means they're likely all females. Hmmm. Since she wants to get rid of the kittens, have Hailey drive down to the Ratchett farm and pick them up. By the sounds of things she won't care what we're doing as long as she gets rid of them. Have her call Mrs. Ratchett and set it up. Tell Hailey she can borrow my truck if she needs to, and the Ratchett farm is the first property on the Welland Road. Insist to Mrs. Ratchett that's what we want to do, not have them delivered here to the clinic."

Dr. Jen was smiling, lighting up her otherwise wane appearance today. "And what are we going to do with five kittens? Are you planning to take them home with you, Beau?"

He chuckled. "No. What I'll do is bring up that big cage from the basement and move a couple of chairs so we can set it up in the far corner of the waiting room. That's where the babies will stay until we adopt them out. I don't want to get into the habit of doing that necessarily, but I've done it before and it worked out. Those kittens won't last long before they're snapped up. But they'll have to be flea checked and examined to see if they're healthy, and we'll have to needle them. They won't be going anywhere until we determine they're okay."

* * *

Hailey was all smiles as she left on her kitten rescue mission and was back in under a half hour with the box of babies. It was a quiet day at the clinic so everyone was gathered around when Beau opened the carton and there inside were five very cute longhaired kittens. Three of the five had a face that was half black and half orange, with yellow eyes on the orange side, and bright blue eyes on the black. One kitten had a black nose and one black ear, again with the same mismatched eyes, and one had two yellow eyes and was predominantly black with orange speckled ears and ruff. Most interestingly, an examination revealed four of the kittens were indeed female but the fifth, the yellow-eyed kitten, was a male calico.

Hailey was handling the kittens, the male ready to do mock battle as he reared back dramatically and boxed with her fingers. "Remind me again, Beau, why a male calico cat is so rare."

"It's all about the chromosomes," he explained. "Two X chromosomes are needed to make a calico, and that would be a female thing because male cats only have one X and one Y. So that means that little kitten you're holding is a very rare XXY. And because that's a genetic anomaly, those males are usually sterile. You see a male in about one out of every 3,000 calicos."

Veterinary assistant Nancy Sweet was eyeing the kittens. "Do we have to adopt them out?" she asked. "We could take them ourselves. I know I'd like to. My cat, Spidey, needs a friend to play with."

Beau smiled. He kind of figured they'd never make it to the cage in the corner. They'd all find homes among the staff, and he was right.

Hailey Cruickshank laid claim to the male calico, Dr. Jen took two, Nancy took one to keep Spidey company, and Melanie

Pearson the other vet tech spoke for the fifth. All in all it was a good morning's work, because the animals had been saved and found excellent homes.

Beau let them have some time with the kittens before they had to get back to work. Since there weren't any scheduled appointments for another half hour it would be a great opportunity to get the little balls of fluff needled with their first immunizations.

He caught Hailey's eye as she was putting her kitten back in the cardboard pet carrier from the supply out back. "Can I speak with you for a moment, Hailey?"

"Sure, Beau," she said as she put some kitten kibble in the box along with a hand knit toy she'd purchased from the counter display, then made her way into his office.

"What were your impressions at the Ratchett farm?" he asked once she was seated. "Anything jump out at you?"

Hailey nodded solemnly. "I was waiting to speak to you about that. Inspectors need to go out there right away, Beau. First of all the place is a mess, junk everywhere which only matters I suppose if you're doing a piece for Outstanding Farms & More, but a lot of the stuff is in with the animals. Not a lot of room left for green space. I saw a couple of horses standing down in a corner of what was supposed to be a pasture, and in my opinion they were much too thin. I could see ribs. And there was this big cage with dogs in it. I couldn't get a good look at them. I was in and out of there quickly because she had the box of kittens ready for me and met me in the yard. I got the impression she wanted me out of there right away. It was no doubt a toss up which she wanted more, to get rid of the kittens or not have anyone come in there. She seemed very nervous the whole time I was there."

Beau listened intently, knowing where his next phone call was going. "I'm surprised she didn't do away with the kittens herself."

Hailey nodded. "She must have been attached to them and couldn't bring herself to do it, thank heavens. It could have soothed her conscience thinking they would be humanely destroyed."

"About those dogs. How big was the cage?"

"It was like an extra large kennel for a big dog like a Newfoundland or a Saint Bernard."

"And how many dogs were in there?"

"They were jumping around so much it was hard to see, but too many for the size of the enclosure. I'd say there were at least three dogs in that thing, not big ones, but it was crowded."

Beau puffed a sigh. "Anything else?"

"Not really. It makes you wonder why such conditions exist. Why people think it's okay to treat an animal that way."

"Believe it or not most of these situations are created by animal lovers. They want to give unwanted pets a home and then people start bringing them everything from goats to guppies and they quickly become overwhelmed. They can't say no, so before long they find themselves in an animal-hoarding situation. It's sad, but it's not about people's feelings, it's always about the safety and welfare of the animals. Someone has to speak for them. In this case these guys are farmers and ought to know how to take care of their animals."

"I think Mrs. Ratchett is a good person...."

"Is she all alone out there do you think?"

"I believe her husband died a few years ago, but she has three grown sons who live there with her. They'd be the ones taking care of everything."

He nodded. "I have to wonder how many animals you didn't see. Chances are that house is full of cats. Anyway, thanks for the information. This will be taken care of today, I can assure you."

* * *

It was late when he locked up the clinic and started for home, and the work that waited for him there. It'd been in the back of his mind all day that he should go up to the movie location and look around. He'd like to meet the wolf dogs, but they weren't supposed to be on set for another week or so, unless the director rearranged his shooting schedule. In that case he would have been notified.

Nigel Garretson was a character, but he was top shelf all the way when it came to the quality of his work and the care he took with animals. A person who loved animals couldn't be all bad in his opinion. The director had told him he owned six big dogs back home in Mission Viejo, California, all of whom he adored: a Dogue de Bordeaux, two Irish Wolfhounds and three Great Danes. He and Beau had enjoyed a lively conversation about dogs, but when there was a difference of opinion about training, Nigel had gotten his back up. He was a nice man with a very large chip on his shoulder for whatever reason, and he could see where actors and indeed anyone in the film industry would eventually butt heads with him. He was very conscious of his title as a director, and seemed to enjoy the fact that he would always have the last word. He insisted on it.

But there would be no movie location tonight he thought, disappointed. "Be honest with yourself," he chided himself aloud. "You wanted to see if you could run into Alexandra Martel.”

Now wouldn't that be something. That telephone call had played itself over and over in his mind since last night. It would've been great to have had a longer conversation with her, but she'd bolted when she'd heard Jen at the door. And what had Jen said? *Sorry I'm later than I expected to be* or something like that. Not much wonder Alexandra had hung up, she'd assumed he was in a relationship and promptly exited an awkward situation. He didn't blame her. Jen had no idea the damage she'd done, and he was not about to tell her because she felt bad enough as it was. No need to rub her nose in it.

He'd love to have the chance to talk to Alexandra again, but what would he say? The situation *was* awkward. No way around that. Tomorrow he'd find the time to go up to the location, or if he was very lucky, the director would call and request his presence on set. Then he'd be almost certain to run into the striking actress. He'd get this misunderstanding straightened out right away.

His mind returned to the events of today. He'd checked with the SPCA inspectors who'd gone out to the Ratchett farm shortly after he'd alerted them to possible animal abuse or neglect. The results had not been good. They found seven horses that needed to be removed from the farm because they were substantially underweight. There was a dead pig in the barn, four goats that were considered at risk and nine dogs that were slightly underweight but inhumanely housed in cramped cages. They were also taken from the premises. Surprisingly there were only three cats in the house, and they were in good condition, two females and one male. All were taken away with Mrs. Ratchett's permission to either be neutered or spayed by a cat rescue organization, and eventually returned to the elderly woman.

As some of these things went it wasn't horrible, there'd been much worse, but even one animal suffering was one too many. In any event, Mrs. Ratchett would apparently escape prosecution because she did not look after any animals except the cats. Her three sons on the other hand were all facing charges with respect to the livestock and dog violations. It seemed the Ratchett brothers were uncooperative and had threatened the inspectors, so it had been necessary to involve the police. That would result in further charges. It had been most fortuitous for the animals involved that Mrs. Ratchett had called the clinic about those kittens. Perhaps she'd known all along it would bring about a much-needed inspection of the family farm.

* * *

Alexandra stretched luxuriously in her comfy bed before swinging her legs to the floor and hitting the shower. There were several scenes being shot today, minor ones that would contribute to the overall storyline, and two pivotal scenes as Nigel referred to them. The one she was dreading the most was the kissing scene. She'd always gotten by before with the old tried and true method of cupping the other actor's face and then either actor sliding their thumb over the lips so there'd be no actual contact. It looked real when you saw it back. It began with the slow, calm approach, the intimate eye contact, all key so both actors knew when it was going to happen.

Nigel Garretson took a different view of things, making it clear to both she and James there would be no shortcuts with the kissing scenes. The same rules would apply when it came to their bedroom scene. No actual sex would take place, but it would be the next thing to it, Nigel had stressed.

With rehearsal and the actual takes, she'd have to kiss James several dozen times. Not that he wasn't a handsome, desirable man, but he was James Langford and everything about the man turned her off. He was too pretty, too sure of himself, too delusional about his effect on the opposite sex. He assumed every woman was panting

144

after him. He'd found out differently with her though and that's the way it was going to stay.

Makeup was a breeze today, no need to cover dark circles from lack of sleep. She'd slept like a log last night and looked vibrant and clear-eyed this morning. That should earn her some much-needed points with Nigel.

She was relieved that nothing too drastic was required, kiss-wise, during rehearsal. It was the usual fare.

"And Action!"

Alexandra and James did the slow burn from across the room, a mating ritual as old as time, in this case for Hubert and Sari Patton. Hubert was an unhinged man besotted with his wife but bent on punishing her for having had the nerve to leave him despite the fact he'd succeeded in getting her back. Sari was now trapped in this multi-million dollar mansion, his palace. She was terrified of her husband, yet there was still the pull that had brought them together in the first place. He wanted to own her, control her, and she would go along with whatever he demanded in order to coerce him and perhaps win her freedom once and for all.

And then she was in James' arms, his lips upon hers. Ugh! He'd been eating garlic since they'd rehearsed, and she involuntarily gagged.

"Cut!" shouted Nigel, beside her in an instant. "Miss Martel, the script has not changed. You are to be seductive. This man is your husband and no matter what has happened between you two in the past the undeniable chemistry remains. Making a face as you did is not chemistry. It looked as though you were about to vomit."

Alexandra straightened her dress and threw back her shoulders. "He ate garlic," she said by way of explanation. "The smell of garlic, especially on somebody's breath, makes me gag."

Nigel's gaze fell upon James, then immediately swung back to her. "Miss Martel, I doubt Mr. Langford ate garlic just to upset you. You remember what acting is, do you not? It is pretending. It is transporting yourself to another plane. It is achieving the best performance possible no matter what the circumstances. What actors must endure to deliver a prize-winning performance is legendary. One does what one must do. In this case you are to enjoy the taste of garlic. Tell yourself it is delicious, and you will quickly come to believe it. Now, we will try again."

And try again they did but her aversion to garlic showed on her face no matter how stoic she tried to be. James was loving it, chuckling at her reaction. She couldn't understand why Nigel was putting up with it.

Finally after several more spoiled takes, Nigel offered James some strong breath mints and once he'd had a chance to chew a few they resumed shooting.

That was better, but by the end of the day she couldn't help but feel violated. James Langford was a pig and took advantage at every opportunity. Those kisses had been nothing short of erotic and this was just one of many kissing scenes scheduled to take place between the onscreen married couple.

It had been hours before Nigel got the shot he wanted, and they were ready to move on.

"Hey, doll face, that was some kiss," said James as he loped up to her later. "I knew you had it in you. You're some kisser when you get down to it."

He winked at her as he walked away and she rolled her eyes, trying to shake him off. The thoughts of that deep invasive kiss made her want to gag all over again. Of all the acting experiences she'd had so far she had never felt such an aversion to another human being. She'd been trying to talk herself out of those feelings since the day they met, but she'd so far been unsuccessful.

Filming went on well into the evening and when she finally made it back to her trailer she was completely exhausted. The first order of business was a nice long soothing shower, then a Swiss cheese on rye sandwich before it was time to go over her lines for tomorrow.

She thought again about Dr. Remington, or Beau as he'd said to call him. She'd love to call him Beau if their paths ever crossed again, but it was obvious after that uncomfortable conversation, he wasn't available. But she could have sworn his antenna was up when they'd met, way up. A woman usually wasn't wrong about something like that. He might have been a little star struck, there was always that possibility, but he could also be a player. If there was anything that shut a woman down fast, it was a fool around type of guy. No thank you no matter how good-looking he was. Beau Remington was handsome *and* sexy, heavy on the sexy. The camera would love him.

Now take James by comparison. As far as she was concerned he was a non-starter because he was too aware of his good looks. He made no secret of the fact he thought he was all that and more, but one thing he wasn't, was sexy. Kissing him today was like kissing a dead fish. Cold, slippery … terrible! Before she'd taken her shower she had brushed her teeth for five minutes but couldn't seem to get the taste of him out of her mouth. That there would be much more of the same during the next few weeks was almost too much to bear.

She thought about kissing Beau. "Isn't that just perfect," she mused aloud. "I'm fantasizing about someone I'll never have because he's married," but he did look like he would be a very good kisser. The thought of it made her heart skip a beat. No matter, they were not destined to be together.

A knock at her trailer door startled her, but when she opened it there stood her personal assistant, Pam.

"Come on in, Pam," Alexandra welcomed her.

"I got that laundry done for you this morning," her assistant told her, "and cleaned up in here a little bit. Anything else you need me to do tomorrow?"

"There is. I was going to make a list before I went to bed but now you're here I can tell you what I want. I'm going to need a few things at the supermarket. I guess you'll have to drive all the way into Hampton so I'd say buy larger quantities that'll hold me for a while, but I'd like some oat cultured yogurt and a large bag of raw walnuts. I should have brought those with me, but I forgot, and two or three dozen plain bagels and two or three packages of Swiss cheese. Also a large container of olive oil margarine, a flat of spring water, and oh yes, a few cans of Italian Wedding Soup. I love that stuff, oh and fresh vegetables."

Pam was busily jotting the items down in her notebook. "Anything else? Some berries? Bananas? Golden Delicious apples? You love those. Mangoes? Papaya?"

Alexandra laughed. "You have a great memory. Yes to all of that. I like lots of variety. I think the market in Hampton is quite small so you might not get mangoes or papayas there. You'll have to go into Franklin for those, but whatever you can get will be very much appreciated."

Pam looked up. "I won't come back without any of it."

Alexandra sighed. "Wonderful, and one more thing. It's my grandmother's birthday tomorrow so I'll need you to send her a nice arrangement. She likes pink roses so make it a monochromatic colour scheme. I'll leave it to you to make the final choice because you have excellent taste. Sign my name and say lots of love to the world's best grandmother, which she is."

She provided Pam with her grandmother's address for delivery, and on a whim told her to add a bottle of pink champagne. Fit it into the arrangement somehow. Grandmother Bridger would get a kick out of that.

"Anything else?"

Alexandra thought for a moment. "There is. Buy yourself some nice flowers and don't skimp."

Pam smiled. "Thank you, Alexandra. I appreciate your thoughtfulness. Anything else?"

Alexandra shook her head. "That's fine. Thank you for taking care of all that. Now I'll let you go so you can get some sleep."

Pam laughed. "I won't be turning in for a while. A bunch of the crew are getting together tonight, and I've been asked to join them. I'll see you tomorrow."

** * **

It was after a long leisurely horseback ride that Beau remembered a couple of veterinary medical journals that had arrived in the mail today. He'd meant to bring them home with him from the clinic to read before he went to sleep, so after cooling young Chance down he jumped in his pickup and headed for the office.

He found what he was looking for in his in-basket and was locking the door behind him on the way out, when three men stepped out of the shadows.

Chapter 8

The first punch landed squarely on the side of his head knocking him off balance. But he got his feet under him and kept from going down, moving quickly into position for whatever might come at him next in the dark. He didn't need to wonder who it was. It had to be the Ratchett brothers.

Backing further into the parking lot under the glow of the dusk to dawn light, he finally got a good look at his opponents. Not much wonder they'd needed to rely on a sucker punch, they looked like they would use every dirty trick in the book. Ranging in height from about five foot seven to about five-nine, what they lacked in size and finesse, they made up for in numbers. Three against one was not a fair fight, but then again farmers who'd starve their animals didn't have much fairness in them.

He didn't know their names, just that they were mean looking as they circled him like a pack of hungry wolves. He figured he was in for a beating before this whole thing was over.

Beau pivoted, trying to keep his eyes on all three. It was an impossible task and the kick to the back of his thigh that sent him sprawling onto the ground served to underline that fact.

"Get 'im, Joey," yelled the brother who'd delivered the kick, triumphant he'd brought the big man down and anxious to have another brother inflict more damage. "Put the boots to 'im."

Before Beau could scramble back to his feet, Joey delivered a bone-rattling kick to his hip that sent shock waves through his entire body. Despite his pain he managed in a lightning move to grab Joey's foot and bring him down onto his backside with a resounding thump. That brother's roar of pain verified he hadn't enjoyed the takedown. He was slow to get up, which gave Beau the advantage he needed as he leapt to his feet.

The adrenalin was pumping when he faced the two who were still standing, glancing back momentarily to make sure the third brother hadn't yet shaken off his inglorious landing.

That split second gave the first brother the opportunity to land a blow he never would have been able to had Beau not been trying to watch all three. He'd give that brother credit for what under any other circumstances could be a knockout uppercut. There was a lot behind that punch, and it felt as though his eye had been dislodged from its socket. Stars exploded inside his skull.

Beau lashed out and connected with a chin that could have belonged to either of the two standing Ratchetts, considering how they were ducking and diving. Obviously practiced brawlers, they'd been good and ready for this fight.

Headlights pierced the darkness, the vehicle slowing as it approached the clinic. Whoever it was, their arrival was a Godsend.

All three brothers were now on their feet but backing off fast. "You keep your nose out of other people's business," one of them warned Beau. "You're going to get more of what you got tonight if you make any more trouble."

And with that all three raced toward the back exit from the parking lot and up to the main road. Seconds later a half-ton truck fired to life and squealed away from the curb.

Winded, Beau staggered toward the back door and slid down the wall to sit on the asphalt as Jen ran up, dropping to her knees in front of him.

"Beau, what happened? What did those men want?"

He tried to smile. "They wanted to hurt me, and they got in some mighty good licks. Here, I'll let us in," he said as he started to get up. "I want to wash some of this blood off my face. The guy must have been wearing a ring because there's a cut under my eye, I can feel it."

"Beau, this is terrible! You take it easy, I've got my keys right here in my pocket," she told him, and she had the door unlocked and the light on as he finished standing up.

That punch to the face had rung his bell as he found a chair in the waiting room and slumped into it.

"Beau, you're a mess," she said, kneeling in front of him again. "Here, you stay right where you are, and I'll get some wet paper towels. We'll get that blood washed off and then I'll get an icepack out of the freezer for your eye."

He wanted to laugh but it would hurt too much. The pain was ridiculous although he doubted anything was broken. Nevertheless, the way his hip was throbbing the jury might still be out on that one. He'd be stiff and sore tomorrow.

She hurried back with the icepack and wet towels and began to clean his face.

"Thanks, Jen," he said taking the towels from her, "but there's no need to fuss over me. I'm okay, just a little ragged around the edges. Thanks for this though. Can you grab an icepack for my left hip? I took a hard shot there, I'd say from steel-toed boots."

She was back in seconds with another icepack. "Okay, Beau, this is me as a doctor talking now, well a veterinarian. Undo your pants or let me do it so I can get this icepack inside where it'll do the most good."

That's what needed to happen so he undid his jeans, adjusted his boxer briefs accordingly and she slid the pack into place before he sat back down, his left leg stretched out in front of him.

"It's good to get ice on that," she said, "because it's already swelling and probably discolouring. Any other injuries?"

"The back of my leg, but I'll get to that later."

"It looked like there were three of them."

"There were."

"They were waiting for you here? Hiding too, I'll bet."

"Right and right again. Likely saw my truck and decided to surprise me when I left."

He flexed the leg that'd been kicked. It was minimally painful at the moment, but he could feel his hip tightening up fast. He wouldn't be surprised if his bursa was ruptured, but if that's all it was it would heal up easily enough.

"Where else did they get you?" she asked, leaning over him.

"The eye as you can see. I also took a punch to the side of my head, but boy those morons liked to kick."

"Who would do such a thing, Beau? You do so much good in the community, always helping other people. Who were they for heavens sake?"

Beau tried to smile but fell short of the mark. "They didn't get around to introductions, but it doesn't take a genius to figure out it was the Ratchett brothers. It would be just about their speed to ambush a man. They warned me not to make any more trouble for them."

"Do you want me to call the police?"

He was already shaking his head. "No police. It was only a couple of punches. I'll live. They've let me know how they feel and that could be the end of it. We'll see what happens next, if anything."

"Beau! You have to call the police," she pleaded. "They might try to kill you next time."

"I doubt there'll be a next time, but I want to leave it alone for now. Okay?"

She was visibly upset. "No, it's not okay!"

"I'm the one with the bruises and I say I'm leaving it alone for the time being. I don't want to make more of this than necessary, create a war over one short battle."

"But Beau...."

"End of discussion." He looked up at her. "Why were you coming here this time of night?"

She smiled despite her concern. "Remember what I was saying about men being so stubborn? Case in point, but like you say they're *your* bruises. Why was I coming here this time of night? I could ask you the same thing. You're not usually here at night."

He tried to pull a face, but like the smile, it wasn't going to happen. "I forgot to take home those journals that came in the mail today. I figured I'd get some reading done tonight, but if I do manage I'll be doing so with one eye. And you never answered my question."

She smiled. "There's that old serendipity again. You can believe this, or you don't have to, but I happened to be driving by on my way home when I noticed your vehicle in the parking lot. I never saw what was going on until I drove into the yard. Here, let me take a look at that," she said nudging his hand aside that was holding the icepack and using her other hand to tilt his head. She looked closely at the injury. "Beau, you are going to have a shiner! It's already turning purple."

He gently eased his head out of her cupped hand, "Great. At least that's the only visible injury."

She chuckled. "Are you going to tell everyone what happened?"

He was silent for a moment. "I haven't thought about that yet."

"And you have to go up and work on that movie looking like you do. They're going to wonder who you were rumbling with."

He flexed his hip. He'd have to get up and start moving or he wouldn't be able to put any weight on that side at all.

"Luckily I'm not going to be in front of the cameras, so it doesn't matter," he said. "Besides, I'll take working behind the scenes any day of the week."

She dabbed at the cut under his eye because it had begun to leak again. "Beau, the camera would love you. And if you were in the movie and you had a fight scene, you'd be perfect."

He pulled his head away. "No more fight scenes for a while thanks," he said as he got up and began to move around, taking the ice from his hip and setting both gel-packs on a side table. "Thanks for all of this, Jen, but there's nothing more going on here tonight so you may as well continue on home."

She shook her head. "I'm not going anywhere until I know you're all right. I'm serious."

"I'm all right."

"There's a clinic down in Hampton. I can call them and tell them we're on our way and get you looked at by a doctor. I think that would be the wise thing to do here."

"Thanks for your concern, but I'm fine. It was a few punches. I'm tougher than I look. Now you drive on home. I'll go find those journals where I dropped them out in the yard and then do the same thing."

"Do you need some help getting home? You might not feel so good once you're behind the wheel."

He tried another smile. "No, Jen, but thank you. I'm fine. I'm going to ice my hip again as soon as I get home. I'll take a couple of painkillers for this headache and be as good as new in the morning. So goodnight, I'll see you in the a.m."

"All right then. I'll see you in the morning and if you're not up to coming in I don't mind taking care of your appointments. Just let me know."

"I'll be fine," he reassured her, heading for the parking lot before she could protest further.

Whoever Jen ended up with in her life, and he had no doubt she'd find a husband faster than she supposed she would, he'd be well taken care of.

* * *

Once he'd taken a shower, popped a couple of over the counter painkillers and got an icepack on his hip, he started to feel much better and made it all the way through the first publication before he fell asleep. It was two in the morning when he woke up, the icepack now thawed and wet, the journal laying on his chest and Ajax licking his hand for a middle of the night trip outdoors.

It was almost three o'clock by the time he got settled down again and he was pleased his headache had eased to the point where it was tolerable. He'd leave it at that if it hadn't returned with a vengeance by morning. He wasn't a pill popper so the less he could get away with the better. He'd taken a look at his eye in the bathroom mirror and wasn't surprised at how bad it looked. Whichever brother had struck him there had really unloaded, but it wasn't the first black eye he'd ever had.

He'd been ten when he'd gotten into a schoolyard scrap with Cameron Reynolds, the school bully. Reynolds was half a head taller and three years older than he was, but he'd handled himself well despite the punches he'd taken. What was more important, Cameron didn't try to bully him anymore because he'd stood up to him. He had no stomach for bullies. He remembered the look on his father's face when he'd come home from school that day. His father had scolded him for fighting, but Beau could tell he'd understood why he'd done it. His mother had been a whole different matter, and he'd had no choice than to let her fuss over him a bit, her only child. One thing was for sure though, he'd forgotten how much it hurt to be on the receiving end of a punch.

* * *

The next day dawned a muted peach and pink masterpiece, but then it quickly clouded over and threatened rain. That meant the outdoor scene to be shot in the garden might not take place, but by noon the sun reappeared, and everything would go ahead as scheduled.

Alexandra was in her typical upbeat mood today, vowing that not even Nigel Garretson or James Langford would ruin it

163

for her. Unfortunately Nigel walked around under a black raincloud at all times, and James seemed to like nothing better than to get after her. She suspected that's the way he'd act with whomever didn't fall at his feet after he'd dazzled them with his charm. She couldn't imagine why he still had that axe to grind seeing as how everyone was talking about the production assistant who was sneaking into his trailer every night. It was the poorest kept secret on Belleisle Bay.

"There you are, doll face," she heard from behind as she stepped outside her trailer. Speak of the devil she thought.

"Good morning, James," she said with a stiff smile.

"All ready to light the world on fire today with your dazzling thespian skills? Few are your equal when you get behind a scene. We're talking Oscar nomination for sure."

She resisted the urge to roll her eyes. James was so full of it he squeaked when he walked or should.

"Thank you for the vote of confidence," she said over her shoulder. "I appreciate it."

"I'm serious," he said finally catching up with her. "You're very good, Alexandra, and I wanted you to know I'm not sorry I recommended you for this picture. You've proved me right over and over again, so thank you."

She'd never met anyone who ran as hot and cold as he did, but she'd made up her mind to go with the flow, whichever way that might be.

"Like I said, thank you. I appreciate the vote of confidence."

"And it's important we work together for the common goal. This is going to be a big picture."

"Work together for the common goal. Does that mean no more garlic?"

"I have Greek blood in my veins, darlin'. I like my spicy food. But from now on I'll take it easy on the garlic and save myself for you."

To her credit she kept the smile on her face. "Thank you, I...." was all she got out before noticing none other than Dr. Beau Remington walking toward Nigel who was standing off to the side of the mansion, in animated conversation with the executive producer.

Stopping in her tracks she did a double take, her heart speeding up accordingly. She caught herself gaping before she brought everything under control and tried to look away. James stopped beside her, following the path of her gaze. Given his fragile ego, he wasn't pleased he'd caught her gawking at the handsome veterinarian.

"So that's the way it is, is it?" he asked, instantly switching to heavy sarcasm. "And here I thought we were going to start getting along better. All right, Miss Martel, game on," and with that he strode away to where the production assistant was watching him with eagle eyes.

Alexandra didn't bother to reply and wondered if anyone ever guessed there was often more drama behind the scenes in moviemaking than there ever was onscreen. When you brought this many people together for a common purpose you were bound to have differences of opinion, attraction to one another and any of a dozen other scenarios.

It was obvious to see from where she was standing that Beau had one heck of a shiner. That hadn't been there the last time she'd seen him. And then an awful thought occurred to her, and she instinctively hoped she was wrong. Had her call somehow angered his spouse and she'd poked him in the eye? No! She was beginning to think like some of the characters from the scripts she'd performed, but she was curious as to what had happened.

She watched as Beau and the director shook hands by way of greeting, and suddenly remembering she was standing in the middle of the yard watching him, made herself scarce. There was absolutely no point of getting in a dither about someone who was not available. She could not remember when she'd felt such an attraction, and it was her poor luck he'd be married or in the very least spoken for. Considering how attractive he was, it was not hard to understand. The man was gorgeous.

"A penny for your thoughts," Gloria the makeup artist joked with her later. "You're looking serious today, Alexandra. You're going to have frown lines if you're not careful."

Alexandra smiled. "And if I were over the moon happy I'd have laugh lines, smile lines, so which is worse?"

"Good point. I heard your sisters were here to see you the other day. Everyone is talking about how there are two more of you. I'll bet you guys had a lot of fun playing pranks on people when you were growing up."

Alexandra shrugged. "I don't recall us playing pranks on people. We were quite serious kids, all I remember contending with was the frustration of people getting us mixed up with one another."

"And you're all identical."

"Umm hmmm. Identical."

"Has the director spoken to you about that?"

"Nigel? Why would he speak to me about that?"

"I don't know, I thought he'd want to cast all three of you in something."

Alexandra chuckled. "I'm thinking most days Nigel is glad there's only one of us to contend with and not three."

"He can be hard to get along with."

The last thing Alexandra wanted to participate in was gossip, and it ran rampant in situations like these. Sometimes wherever people were gathered the temptation for tittle-tattle was irresistible.

"He's a perfectionist and I guess his track record speaks for itself."

"So you like working with him?"

"I was very honoured to be chosen for this movie."

"Are you and James Langford an item?" Gloria pressed, not getting the hint. "I see him panting after you all the time like a little puppy dog. He's been married several times you know. The way he looks at you I'd say he's sizing you up to be the next Mrs.

Langford. It must be nice to look like you do."

How did she answer that one! "I'm not looking to make a change in my marital status, Gloria. I try to keep everything strictly professional."

'Yeah, right,' her conscience reminded her as she remembered her late-night call to Beau. But that call had backfired and so she *would* keep it professional from now on, she thought, still feeling the sting of discomfiture.

Gloria lowered her voice conspiratorially. "It must be heaven to kiss James Langford though."

'Heaven!' she thought. Hardly, but aloud she said: "It was a routine kissing scene."

"But you got to kiss James Langford, I mean it doesn't get any better than that, does it?"

Alexandra sighed, keeping her face still as Gloria applied lip colour. By the time she'd finished, Alexandra had her pat answer ready. "I don't kiss and tell," she winked and since her makeup was complete, she thanked Gloria for her usual job well done and luckily the call to set came before she could be questioned further.

* * *

169

Alexandra had considered going for a run at the end of shooting today. She wouldn't go far because it had been another demanding day, but a run would help clear her head. The trouble was, it was threatening to rain again, and she didn't want to get caught out. She could easily hop in the car with the security guy who she knew would insist on following her when she ran, but that wasn't the way she wanted to finish a good run.

No she would go for a run tomorrow and was pleased to put that plan in place. She wouldn't make arrangements with security though because she wanted to do it by herself.

Now back to work, she mused, corralling her thoughts. She'd almost finished going through her scenes for the next day when her cellphone rang. She knew it wouldn't be Beau by some miracle of divine intervention, not after being blocked. She was happy to see it was Naomi on the other end of the line.

"Hi, Sis!" she chirped. "How are things on the ranch?"

Naomi sighed. "Busy as usual. Hayden watches over me like a mother hen while he works *himself* to death, I might add. But that's the way he wants it."

"Everything's okay isn't it?"

"Oh sure! The reason I'm calling is that Hayden and I have decided on a name for our little boy."

"Drum roll please."

"Okay, it's Bridger."

"Bridger! After Grandmother Bridger. Naomi it's perfect! I never even thought of that, but Gram must be over the moon about you guys wanting to name your baby after her. Bridger Barlowe. I love it. What have you come up with for a middle name?"

"That's where we differ a little. I want Lee because I think it flows better, Bridger Lee Barlowe. Don't you think that's a good combination?"

"It does flow, and I like it. I can see that name in lights. But you said you and Hayden differ. So what's his choice?"

"He wants Bridger Duke Barlowe."

Alexandra was silent for a moment. "Hmmm. It is a mouthful, but I can see Hayden wanting that name because it would be for his grandfather."

"That's right, that's why I'm not saying much other than the original protest. I'm so thankful Hayden has made peace with everything that happened between him and his grandfather to where he'd even think about using his name. It's all good."

"I agree. What does Ginger think about your choice?"

"She's like you. She thinks it's awesome that Hayden has let all of that bad stuff in the past go and moved ahead."

"Will he go by Duke or Bridger?"

"Bridger I would say. Bridger Barlowe. The more I say it the better I like it. And in a few weeks we'll be holding our little boy in our arms. We're so excited to become parents it's unbelievable. It can't come soon enough to suit me. I'm not looking forward to going through the delivery since Ginger had such a hard time, but millions of women do it every day and so will I."

"Where is the *Daddy* right now?" asked Alexandra.

Alexandra loved the change in her sisters' voices when they spoke about their husbands. That's what she wanted someday, notwithstanding that the only prospect on the horizon now was the insufferable James Langford. Someday she'd meet the man of her dreams, although it was looking more and more like she was going to be alone for the rest of her life.

"Hayden was exhausted, so he went up to bed. He'll be sleeping like a log by the time I get up there"

"That's sexy."

"Very. He usually wakes up when he hears me getting into bed. Alexandra, are you sure you can't see yourself with that good-looking actor, James Langford? He's so handsome and obviously smitten with you. Ginger and I want you to have what we have some day. We're so happy and we want you to be happy too."

"Then don't match me up with James Langford. Marital happiness and James Langford don't belong in the same sentence. Besides, I am happy. Acting fulfills me. I won't say that every day is peachy keen, but I'm doing what I want to do so don't worry about me. Okay?"

"All right, point taken. Okay, that's all the news I have. Now I'm going to let you go and get your beauty sleep, and I'll get mine. Love you!"

"Love you too!"

* * *

Beau was in the middle of a memorable dream, when the phone on his bedside table woke him.

"Beau, this is Jen! You need to come down to Hatfield Point immediately!" she told him urgently. "The clinic is on fire!"

Chapter 9

Dropping the phone unceremoniously he grabbed his jeans from a nearby chair, a T-shirt from the dresser draw and jammed his feet into boots. He snatched up his truck keys and raced outside, zipping himself up as he ran. He barely felt the pain in his hip and leg through the massive adrenalin surge.

The volunteer fire department was already on the scene. To his everlasting relief it looked as though they had already doused the flames although they continued to pour water on the back of the building, the portion of the structure where the nonflammable supplies were stored. The veterinary pharmaceuticals and hazardous chemicals were stored properly in another part of the clinic and thankfully away from the actual site of the fire, otherwise the situation could have been much worse. The oxygen onsite alone could react explosively.

There was also an ambulance on scene. He parked his truck and was jumping out when Jen ran up to him.

"Apparently the guy who started the fire, also caught himself on fire," she announced breathlessly. "I don't think he's hurt too bad but he's hollering up a storm back there."

Indeed he could hear somebody yelling as he trotted over to recognize thc Ratchett brother who'd given him the black eye. Jen was right. It didn't appear as though he was too badly injured, but the burns on his legs did look painful. One hand was burned as well. There was no reason to doubt all three brothers had been involved. Two had fled and left this guy to face the music alone. This was one crime that was already solved.

The brother noticed Beau had joined the group of spectators. "You had this coming, Remington!" the grubby looking young man shouted, clearly furious. "You deserved it."

Beau knew he could say the same thing about him but held his tongue as the paramedics treated the injured man before lifting him onto a gurney.

The guy was spitting mad. "You wait and see what happens next! Who do you think you are, sending those guys out to our farm? You or anyone else comes anywhere near our place and we finish all this," he shouted, including everyone in his remarks.

He could still be heard yelling at the top of his lungs after being loaded into the back of the ambulance. One of the paramedics climbed in beside him and closed the back doors before the vehicle started away.

There were plenty of onlookers for the fiery spectacle, and he was grateful the volunteer fire department was housed such a short distance away. A fire service routinely praised for its dedicated volunteer firefighters, he would personally thank them for saving his clinic with their quick action. He was thankful as well there were no overnight patients staying at the clinic, as was the case from time to time. In the event there were animals that could not go home for one reason or another, somebody was always there to monitor them throughout the night. In a situation such as this there would have been plenty of time to get them safely outside. Still, it would've been a traumatizing experience for them. It showed once again those Ratchett brothers had no compassion at all for animals, either in their own care or anybody else's. Humans either for that matter.

But oh the mess of this place now! Thankfully as the smoke continued to clear it became apparent the fire had consumed very little of the building, but there had to be significant smoke and water damage. They'd be out of business for the next couple of weeks until everything could be cleaned up and repairs made. But he told himself too that things usually looked worse in the moment than they turned out to be, and he clung to that hope.

It wasn't long before the fire chief declared the fire completely extinguished and the men and women departed with their equipment.

Jen was in tears as she surveyed the clinic, a sorry sight now under the glow of street lighting. She turned to Beau. "And all because you wanted to make sure there were no animals being abused on that farm. I'll never understand how people can let animals live, and die, in those conditions and then retaliate when someone tries to help the poor things. If you hadn't sent those inspectors, Beau, there might have been even more animals dead out there. And how do we know how many others have died over the years and been buried on the property. We don't, and never will. What happened here tonight is shocking, but you absolutely did the right thing by ordering that inspection."

He nodded, arms folded across his chest, still not able to pull his eyes away from the blackened back portion of the clinic. "I know. It's hard to understand. They can't see beyond their own selfishness. I think it's because some people view animals as chattel, possessions, and their only value to them is what they can give back. If they're old or sick, they don't care about them anymore. In this case we're talking about young animals in their care that didn't have much of a chance. Put one of these guys in a cage and withhold food and water and see how much they like it. They'd scream bloody blue murder if that ever happened, but when it's a defenseless animal they don't have any qualms about it. There's something seriously wrong with people who act like that. It's laziness for sure, but a whole lot more. Sometimes it can be a generational thing, like the way they were taught to think about animals or saw animals being treated when they were growing up. Who knows?"

"But at least they were able to remove the ones that could be saved on that farm and give them decent homes."

He nodded again. "At the end of the day that's what it's all about. I was expecting some pushback from them, people who feel entitled to treat their animals any way they see fit with no interference. I have to say I didn't expect them to go this far. That tells you everything you need to know about those guys."

Jen too seemed transfixed by the sight of the still smouldering ruins. "And it shows us too what kind of people they are to leave their own brother behind. He could have been injured much worse, and how do they know he wasn't? But they still ran. Bunch of cowards!"

"He was still full of spit and vinegar though wasn't he? Still threatening me in front of all those witnesses. Not too bright, but then that goes back to what I was saying earlier. Anyway, no use crying over spilt milk. What's done is done. I guess I'll have to stay down here for the rest of the night to make sure we don't have anyone going inside. How did you happen to know about the fire so fast?"

She sighed. "I'm a light sleeper. I heard the sirens and when I looked out my window I saw the glow of the fire, and I knew."

"I'm grateful for the fast heads up. Anyway, the excitement's over for the night and you might as well go on home."

"I could do that," she greed, "get some more sleep then come back for the rest of the night. That way you can get some shuteye yourself before you have to look after your own animals."

He was already shaking his head. "You go on home, Jen. I'll take care of this. I don't want you down here alone in case those other brothers come back and try to finish the job. Thanks though."

"I don't mind. I can take care of myself."

"Thanks, but no. I want to do a little poking around inside and then I'll park over there under those trees and hang around for the rest of the night. There's only a few hours left before daylight anyway. You go home because we'll all have to roll up our sleeves tomorrow. There's going to be lots for everyone to do."

"Okay, if you're sure...."

"I'm sure. Go on, go get some sleep. Hopefully all of the excitement is over for the night."

* * *

Once Jen had left and he'd done a walk around the exterior of the building, he moved his truck to the back of the parking lot where the sweeping boughs of oak trees overshadowed the pavement below. He'd tuck in here for a while and try to get some rest.

It took a few minutes but once he'd managed to get comfortable, the seat tilted back, he felt himself begin to drift off. He didn't think he'd slept very long before he was awakened by a bright light shining in his eyes. He struggled to come fully alert. He got out of the truck as the alley light was switched off.

The Mountie climbed out of his car. "Sorry, Dr. Remington, didn't realize it was you. Sorry to wake you."

"It's okay, Allain. Good to know you've got eyes on this place."

"I would have been down here a lot sooner, but we were tied up for quite a while at a fatal accident out near Henderson Settlement. I heard they got the guy who started this though," he said, glancing back at the ruined portion of the clinic. "I understand it was one of the Ratchetts."

"It was."

"Well, if there was one then all three were involved. They're known to us. I'd say this was in retaliation for the inspection I'm guessing, same thing with your face. Want to tell me about that?"

Beau hesitated for a moment. "Yeah, I've been thinking about that. I was prepared to let it go thinking they'd gotten everything out of their system, but now I'll be along to talk to you guys. I figure all three brothers were involved in this too and obviously the other two ran. That's brotherly love for you, run away and leave the man who got hurt behind. Figured I'd stick around here for the rest of the night in case anyone came by thinking they might go inside and take a look around. The whole back end is open and there's lot in there that can be carried out, such as it is."

Allain nodded. "That's too bad. But at least they were able to save the main part of the building. It's going to take a lot of cleanup."

"Yep, plenty of work ahead but that's why I've got insurance. Me and my staff will clean up what we can. I'll get a crew in here to take care of the worst of it. I want to be up and running again as soon as possible. Gotta pay the bills."

The Mountie hooked his thumbs through the band of his utility belt. "Right. Look, I'm at the end of my shift and on my way home but I'll be on call for the rest of the night. If you need me for anything, call and I'll be here as fast as I can."

After agreeing to do that, Beau got in his truck thinking he'd try for another snooze, but that power nap must have done the trick because he was now wide awake. He found his denim jacket behind the seat and pulled it on against the early morning chill. Moving the seat back further in favour of his long legs, and his injuries, he settled in for a more comfortable position. This would be where he'd stay for the next two or three hours anyway.

His gaze shifted to the rear of the building. He guessed the first order of business was to get that boarded up until it could be rebuilt. It couldn't stay the way it was now. When Jen came back he knew she'd be ready to dive into whatever had to be done and he'd get her started on that while he went home and saw to his animals. Then as soon as it was late enough he'd call

Elmer Pearlon to come and shore up that part of the building. It didn't have to be pretty.

Elmer was a much-loved man in the community, who, despite his seventy-eight years had never lost the love of building things. When it was a project of any size his nephew Bruce worked with him, and he was every bit as talented as his uncle. Hopefully the pair would take on the job of rebuilding the back end of the clinic. But first, his tired brain reminded him, he had to get insurance appraisers out here in the morning to assess the damage before any changes were made. He'd file the claim as soon as he got home.

And then for the umpteenth time, he thought about Alexandra and their all-too-brief telephone conversation. If it weren't for Jen's impromptu visit the other night, who knew how things with Alexandra would have gone. Where it would have gone. There was definitely an attraction between them. He could feel it, and it felt good. But regrettably it had been promptly shut down. He couldn't blame Jen for how things had gone. She hadn't known anything about that. It was one of those things, but it still nettled him.

He smiled to himself. As if a movie actress would be interested in him he told himself realistically, a small town veterinarian. She could have her pick of any man. She even had that movie heartthrob,

James Langford, that ass, panting after her, so what chance did he have. But, he reminded himself yet again, she had called *him*. And then everything had gone south, and it was glaringly apparent by his lack of success in calling her back, he'd been blocked. His latest visit to the set hadn't even produced results. There'd been no sign of her. The way he figured it, unless he stormed basecamp when he figured she'd be there and demanded to see her, which would only work in the movies, there wasn't much hope of having a conversation with her now. There was still the scene with the wolf dogs to look forward to, a scene he knew she was in.

But what would he say if he did have the chance to speak with her again? Tell her he was interested in getting to know her? It was probably closer to the truth that she thought he was a two-timer and wouldn't give him the time of day. He had to figure out a way to get her attention, see if there was anything there other than the initial attraction. If he did get a chance to explain and she stuck her nose in the air and ignored him, at least he'd have his answer. Not worth the trouble. But he had to get that shot, somehow. This thing wouldn't stop eating at him until he did.

* * *

The man checked the clock on the bedside table. Ten after four. Time was running dangerously low. He had to make things happen soon, grab that Martel woman and be done with it. This was not at all how he'd planned for things to go. It had all seemed so simple when everything was still on the drawing board. How hard could it be to get her alone? It was a movie set, not Fort Knox, but then again with the amount of security around the place his job was becoming impossible.

He longed for a cigarette, but as he pulled the pack from his pocket he remembered hotel policy. If he smoked in his room there'd be a hefty smoking fee, one that he couldn't pay. He didn't need the attention brought on him by the police if he tried to get away without settling the bill.

He thought about his cigarette again. It was getting so a man couldn't enjoy a good smoke anymore without being pounced on by the smoking police. He wasn't even supposed to light up in his rental car, but he'd figured that one out. He'd simply made sure the AC was pulling in air from the great outdoors and he kept his window cracked enough to draw out the smoke when he held his cigarette up close to it. What he had to go through for the pleasure of a cigarette.

His cellphone vibrated and he considered not answering it until he saw who it was. Better to try to keep on good terms with those boys than to stick a thumb in their face.

He didn't even have to identify himself. They knew his voice by now. "We're waiting for you," came the sinister drawl he'd come to despise, "and your time is almost up. We want that nice little package in our hands no later than one week from today."

"I told you I'm doing the best I can. It isn't easy. When I do score though, I'll score big so back off. You birddogging me isn't going to work."

"Let me hear you say again you know how this thing works."

"I got it. I'm going to be a dead man if I don't pay."

"Good. You understand. One week."

The line went dead.

* * *

Alexandra was restless. She felt claustrophobic. Awakened early to the sound of birds singing she knew that old familiar pull to get out into the fresh morning air and enjoy a good long run. What could it hurt? She understood the need for security, but they were in the middle of nowhere in New Brunswick, in beautiful Belleisle, a sleepy community of friendly hardworking folks. What if she got ready and went by herself? How angry would Nigel be? Would he even care? Maybe not because nowhere in her contract did it state she couldn't go off for a morning run. After all, she was a big girl and could take care of herself.

The more she thought about it the more convinced she became that was exactly what she would do. Too bad she couldn't carry mace to protect herself in the unlikely event of being harassed by anyone, but she'd checked it out. Pepper spray is illegal in Canada and considered a prohibited weapon. Her assistant had even looked up about hiding a canister of the stuff in her luggage while crossing the border from the US until she found out how seriously border security would take that little trick. She couldn't believe it when Pam told her if she was caught coming into Canada with pepper spray it could mean possible jail time and a criminal record. Ouch! So much for feeling ultra safe while jogging she thought. Besides, if she happened to be caught with it *here* there'd be the same brouhaha. If she kept it in her pocket and was found with it, she could be charged with carrying a concealed weapon. Okay, so no pepper spray.

She looked at the clock again. It was a few minutes before five o'clock and while the sun wouldn't rise for another hour, there was plenty of light outside and basecamp was relatively quiet. What would it hurt to go out for say a half hour. She'd be back by five-thirty at the latest, all snug in her trailer with no one any the wiser. That's it! She was going to do it.

* * *

Beau stepped out to stretch when he saw Jen pull into the parking lot. It was now full light and he'd had enough of sitting in his truck, his hip and leg letting him know it was a bad idea.

The ever-cheerful Jen was all smiles as she made her way over to him, passing him a thermal mug of coffee and a pre-buttered blueberry muffin. He had to smile. Yep, she was going to make some man one heck of a wife and he wished at that moment he had the necessary feelings for her. The truth was, he felt no physical attraction whatsoever, whereas a few minutes with Alexandra Martel had lit him up like a Christmas tree. He took the muffin and coffee, but it was on the tip of his tongue to say he was a few minutes from home and could get something to eat when he got there. He'd quickly thought better of it. It would be rude to refuse such a kindhearted offer.

"I brought some for myself too," she explained. "I thought maybe you didn't want to eat breakfast alone. I know I don't. Company is good. I'd say let's go in the clinic and eat but I don't think that's such a good idea at the moment. We could sit in my car if you want."

He briefly eyed her small car. No comfort there. He looked in the direction of

188

his truck. "Let's sit in my vehicle, a little more room to spare, and thanks for this," he said holding up the coffee and muffin. "I am starved."

They settled in and Beau turned on his XM station to provide background during their impromptu breakfast.

"I came dressed for the job," she announced unnecessarily, referring to the old denims and oversized shirt she was wearing. "What should I tackle first?"

"I'm going to file a claim as soon as I get home, and they can send an appraiser out to take pictures. You could use your phone to get a few shots too to go with whatever they take. You can also start an inventory of what's damaged. I'll help you with that later and get it finalized with a replacement cost value. I already checked the pharmaceuticals and stuff, and nothing has been compromised so that's good. I'm hoping I can hire Elmer Pearlon from over in Springfield to do the repair work, so I'll also have to get in touch with him. Anyway, it shouldn't take very long to get somebody out here. So other than snapping some pictures and working along with that other stuff I'd say stay on the property and handle the curious as they come. Hailey and the others will be along by eight-thirty, and they can help you with that, but wait for the adjuster before you move anything. I should hopefully be back by then."

He took a bite of the blueberry muffin. "These are some good, don't tell me you baked them yourself."

She glowed. "I did, and from scratch I might add. I love to bake. And before you ask, the coffee is made from freshly ground beans. Like it?"

"What's not to like? It's delicious. I tell you, Jen, You're something else. You're going to make some man a helluva wife some day."

She gave him a sideways glance. "Thank you, Beau. You can be like the big brother I never had. That's how I'm trying to look at this whole situation now. You'll have to give me some time to get into the little sister thing though. I'll get there eventually."

He laughed as he nodded his head. "Yes, you're going to make some man a helluva wife."

* * *

Alexandra decided on leggings and a long-sleeved top seeing as how it was a bit chilly in these hills, laced on her sneakers and pulled her hair into a ponytail. A ball cap and sunglasses were the final touches, and she was ready for that early morning run. It was exhilarating to get outside by herself for even a short while. She loved her career, but she missed the freedom of being able to do what she wanted when she wanted to do it. She'd had to make peace with the fact that she was, on most occasions, seen as an investment that must be protected.

She saw someone moving around one of the trailers at the far end of the compound, but she slipped away quickly. Keeping to the edge of the trees so she wouldn't stand out, once she was clear of basecamp off she went in a soul-pounding run down the narrow secondary road. The birdsong itself was rich and luxuriant as she drank in lungfuls of crisp fresh air. The smells of the fields, the flowers, the trees, just nature itself as it was laid before her inviting the warmth of the sun preparing to make its grand entrance above the horizon. Oh how she had missed this.

There was nothing to compare with being in nature, nothing filled up the soul in quite the same way. She usually ran in the city but it in no way compared to this. How she missed her uncomplicated life in New Brunswick. She knew her family loved hearing about her glamourous lifestyle as a movie person, but there was much that was lost too.

She glanced around, feeling completely alone in this splendid New Brunswick garden, because that's what she thought of the beauty surrounding her in Canada's picture province. How could anyone feel this was unsafe? Her misgivings came from the level of security at the movie location and presumed it would include her running off into the countryside by herself. She knew very well it did.

There wasn't even any traffic at this time of the morning, that's what was so wonderful about it. She reached up and took off her sunglasses and secured them on her ball cap, then pulled it lower onto her forehead. Who would recognize her anyway way out here? There wasn't a soul around anywhere to bother her.

* * *

Beau licked his fingers and drained the rest of what was the best cup of coffee in recent memory. Too bad she'd brought just one muffin. But again, uncannily, she read his mind.

"I have more muffins in my car," she announced with a twinkle in her eye. "I could use another one, how about you?"

He shook his head, chuckling. "You've got my number, kiddo. Sure, I'll have another one if it isn't too much trouble. I'd be as big as a barn if I hung around with you for any length of time."

The second muffin went down as easily as the first, as did another cup of coffee from the large thermos she'd brought over to the truck with a smile. When they finished he felt more like crawling into bed and pulling the pillow over his head than he did getting to his chores. But that caffeine was beginning to kick in, so he'd have no problem taking care of what needed to be done.

He raised a hand in a goodbye wave as he pulled out of the parking lot minutes later and started up the road toward his ranch. Those dogs of his would be ready for a watering break by the time he got there, overdue in fact. The horses would be chomping at the bit to get out of the barn and into the pasture.

He'd crested a knoll when he saw someone running along the side of the road. You didn't see too many joggers out this way, so whoever it was stood out. Hmmm, it looked like a tall woman with a long black ponytail, her ball cap pulled down low over her eyes. And then it struck him. It was Alexandra Martel!

Chapter 10

Thunderstruck, he continued on up the road until he was well past her before making a turn. She hadn't even glanced in his direction and that was in his favour, so at least he would have the element of surprise going for him. But he did intend to speak to her because he might never have another golden opportunity like this. That is if she would even talk to him. She might not, but he'd at least try.

She was travelling at an even steady pace, and it was obvious she was a long-time runner by the easy stride she maintained. Some joggers windmilled their way along, looking as though they were fleeing police. It had always amused him how some people could turn the simple act of running into an all out struggle to some sort of imaginary finish line. He'd done quite a lot of running himself when he'd played football in high school, so he had a pretty good idea how it was done correctly. So did she.

He made sure his window was down as he came alongside her, but she kept her gaze straight ahead. No way she didn't see him, so he spoke.

"Good morning," he said.

He'd been tempted to say good morning, beautiful, because it would fit, but that was way too smarmy and totally the wrong foot to get off on. Alexandra Martel did not look like the type to suffer fools gladly.

"I said good morning," he repeated pleasantly and this time she did glance over, and he could tell by the look on her face she remembered him. Thank God.

"Good morning," she replied stiffly, upping her speed a little.

"Alexandra, could you please stop for a moment so we can talk?" he asked reasonably.

"Why do you want to talk to me?"

"Because I didn't get a chance to explain about the other night and I would very much like to do that."

"No explanation necessary. I had the bright idea to call you and it didn't work out. End of story."

"Why didn't it work out? You hung up so fast I didn't get a chance to explain."

"Okay, explain about what exactly? You're obviously married, or in some way committed, so that's fine. No problem with that, but why are you sniffing around me if you're already taken? I'm not interested in being part of any of that."

He laughed, which given the flash of irritation that crossed her face it had been the wrong thing to do.

"I'm not trying to make a fool of you," he said with a straight face. "I only want to...."

"You don't have to make a fool of me," she said not at all breathless despite her pace. "I already did a good job of that on my own. I'm not in the habit of calling men, I felt compelled to do so and it blew up in my face. So please go on your way and leave me alone. We all get only one person, and it looks like you already got yours. Goodbye."

This time she did pick up some serious speed, but he doubted she'd be able to maintain it for any distance. So he accelerated and as he was coming abreast of her she put on the brakes, reversed direction and headed back up the road.

Damn! Luckily there was a driveway up ahead, so he turned the truck and went back the way he came, nudging the gas pedal a little to catch up. In about thirty seconds he was out of here. No way was he going to get into a game of cat and mouse like some teenager. He was in no mood to play footsies, good-looking woman or not, but he did want to get some things said and there might never be another opportunity to do so. He finally came alongside her, but she kept her eyes straight ahead having slipped her sunglasses on. Great, now he couldn't even see her eyes.

"Alexandra, for the record, and you can do with this what you want, I am not married, and I'm not romantically involved with another person. What you heard the other night was my colleague, Dr. Jen Tuttle, who dropped by unexpectedly."

"Does Dr. Tuttle know she's not romantically involved with you?"

"Now she does," he answered honestly.

She kept running, cresting a knoll with ease.

"Alexandra, what do you want me to say? I'm not the type to be struck on some movie star so it's not about that at all. I felt a connection with you when we met the other day and as I say I'd like the chance for us to get to know one another. I kind of get the idea you might feel the same way seeing as how you called me, so what do you say? Can we try to do that? Hit rewind?"

She kept running.

"Okay. Look, I'm not into playing games. It's not my thing at all, so if it's a no then just say no, don't give me the silent treatment.

Say what you want to say, right here and now. If it's no I hit the gas, and you don't ever have to see me again. Look through me on set, which I have the idea you might be good at. If it's yes, then we could go out together sometime. You could come to my ranch if you ever had a free moment, and we could go horseback riding or something. Hang out for a while. Your call."

To his heart's never ending joy, she stopped running. She took off her sunglasses and smiled. Boy did his world light up at the sight of that thousand-megawatt smile.

"Is my number still on your phone?"

He nodded. Never would he erase that, and he doubted he'd ever forget the moment he saw it on the screen.

"Perfect, then I'll unblock you. Now, I am definitely AWOL and about to face some serious strife if I don't get back to my trailer, pronto. Sorry, Dr. Remington, but I've got to go," and with that she started away again.

"Beau!" he called after her. "Call me, Beau!"

"Okay, Beau." She turned around, jogging backwards for a few steps to answer him. "You call me. I'll be free around eight," then turned and disappeared over another knoll, her ponytail wagging in a most tantalizing fashion.

* * *

Beau waited for a shiny black SUV to pass him before he pulled back fully into the travelling lane, his face split in an ear-to-ear smile. Wow, had she told him to call her? If this wasn't a pinch me moment than nothing else would ever qualify. He had a date to call Alexandra Martel, and while he got a kick out of the fact that she was a movie star, the most important thing was that he was highly attracted to her.

He arrived home to find three dogs whining at the back door wanting out. They were good, there wouldn't be any puddles, but he had hoped to be home sooner than this. This was the usual time to get them out so no harm, no foul. If any one of them happened to have an accident, it was no big deal either. He loved his pets and whatever they did would be taken in stride.

Next he went to the barn and let the three Chances out of their stalls and despite old Chance's advancing age he frolicked around the pasture like a three year-old. They were picking up on his happy mood. He imagined they could see it on his face because he hadn't stopped smiling since he'd driven away from Alexandra. Wow! Tonight couldn't come soon enough.

It was crazy though. She'd been parked right here in the front of his brain since the moment he'd met her, and he let his imagination run free. Wouldn't it be something if she became part of his life! He knew that was a very long stretch of the imagination, her being a city girl and a movie star to boot while he was just a country vet. He was also a rancher, albeit on a small scale. He'd love to bring in more livestock, but the truth was his veterinary practice kept him hopping. Now if he had someone to share it with he'd get into it in a big way. That had always been his dream. Anyway, back to more pressing matters.

After grabbing a quick shower and another cup of coffee he sat down and dialed the insurance company and filed a claim. He was assured an adjuster would be onsite within a couple of hours so that was good. At least he could get rocking and rolling with that. Allain, the Mountie, had told him when they'd talked last night that the Ratchett brothers were going to be "shut down fast." It was now a matter of rounding the other two up and charging all three.

His next call was to Elmer Pearlon who was eager to take on the project of fixing the clinic. Perfect. He flexed his shoulders after he hung up. Bad things happened, but that was life. It was all in how you handled it. Like getting his clinic up and running again without delay. Until then he was referring calls to another animal hospital in Norton, a bit of a drive away, but doable in the case of an emergency. That was another thing he would take care of as soon as he got back to the clinic, call all scheduled surgeries for the week and postpone them where possible. Luckily there were only two for later this afternoon, so he'd get in touch with the owners in plenty of time.

He was going out the door when his cellphone rang. It was Randy Booker from the Cloverfield Farm over in Springfield.

"Hi, Doc," said Randy, clearly out of breath. "I hope you're available because I've got a first-calf heifer calving and it's a *big* calf. She got bred too soon because the bull jumped the enclosure. She's in trouble, Doc. I'm trying to do it myself with the comealongs but I haven't been able to budge it. It's a breach birth and I've got legs showing but that calf is stuck. I need your help right away. She's down right now, pushing, and I hope she stays down and doesn't get up and run away from us. That'd make things even harder."

"I'm on my way, Randy. I should be there in about ten minutes or so."

"Thanks, Doc. It's already been too long. We need to get the little fella out right away. I'll keep trying until you get here."

Randy Booker was a man in his late sixties, determined to keep the family farm going. With a good strong set of arms to help him pull, the heifer would hopefully be able to finish birthing her calf. There was no way Randy could do it on his own and time was important in matters such as this. The sad truth was that the calf could already be gone, but then sometimes he'd been pleasantly surprised.

Randy met him at the gate, and they drove down to where the heifer was lying in the pasture. Beau fastened on to the calving chains and with two good strong pulls got the big bull calf out. Both men were delighted when they saw the baby was still alive, but just barely it seemed. After cleaning the face off, Beau tickled the calf's nose with a piece of hay in order to make the baby sneeze, not only to clear his nasal passages but also in an attempt to get the animal breathing.

"Mamma's not getting' up, Doc," said Randy.

"She's exhausted I imagine and hurting, but we'll deal with her in a moment," Beau told him as he began massaging the calf to help stimulate blood flow.

That was something the mother would automatically do with her tongue if she were able. It was vital to begin doing it immediately until the mother recovered enough to continue those ministrations on her own.

"Okay now, Randy," said Beau. "I see the mother is starting to show some interest, so let's step way back and see if she does what she's supposed to do. She's still in pain but I see she's getting up and going to him which is an excellent sign."

They watched as the Hereford slowly got to her feet and gingerly made her way to her baby still lying on the ground, lowering her nose to it.

"She's licking the calf," Beau said quietly, "so that's good. Now if he starts to nurse we're in the home stretch. It was a difficult birth, so he'll have to be watched. If he hasn't started nursing within a couple of hours start getting the colostrum into him, but you already know all about this."

"Sure do," Randy agreed, "but it's been awhile since I've had to deal with a hard birth like this around here. My mammas usually get it done on their own."

They both watched with relief as the calf got unsteadily to his feet and began to wobble about. He did seem to be headed in the right direction. Minutes later he had latched on and was nursing greedily.

"Thank you, Doc. I appreciate you getting here as quickly as you did. You saved both of them."

"No problem. I'm glad I was able to come right away. I think he's going to be okay, but keep an eye on him to be sure," Beau told him, still observing the cow and calf before settling up his bill. "If you have any problems, give me a call and I'll run right back out."

"I heard your clinic caught fire last night. Much damage?"

"It could have been worse. They were able to save most of it. We'll be dealing with smoke and water damage now, but the remaining structure is good. We got lucky. I'll know more after cleanup starts."

"I heard it was no accident, like that shiner you got there. News travels fast."

"I guess it does," Beau told him. "Now give me a call if you need me, but I have to get back. I want to be there when the appraiser arrives."

With a wave of his hand Beau backed out of the driveway, turned and headed toward home for another shower and change of clothes. It was turning out to be one of those days, but nothing could keep the smile off his face today. Tonight he was going to talk to what could turn out to be the woman of his dreams.

* * *

It seemed as though her feet had somehow developed springs, each step effortless. That's the way it felt, Alexandra thought to herself. Feet with wings is how she would describe it. That was the difference between being alive with excitement and feeling ho-hum.

Luckily no one seemed to notice her arrival back at basecamp earlier. She'd slipped as inconspicuously as possible into her trailer and after a quick shower and a light breakfast was ready to start her day. She knew having to spend most of it with James Langford would not dampen her spirits. That was put to the test quickly enough when she left her trailer and ran smack dab into the man himself. She didn't bother to ask why he was hanging around. Today she didn't care.

"My, my, I see a smile," James told her laconically. "Someone must have had a visitor last night. I can always tell what puts a smile on a woman's face. I'm sorry it wasn't me. But don't worry, soon enough it will be."

Poor James, he couldn't seem to make up his mind as to whether he liked her or hated her. Every mood of his seemed to be directly related to how she felt about him at any particular moment. Not a match made in heaven and his temperamental nature would explain why he was so familiar with divorce court. James could never seem to find the perfect woman, doubtless because she hadn't been created yet. The only woman who'd have a chance at succeeding with him would be someone who was an extension of himself. Like so many narcissistic men, they wanted a female version of themselves.

"Dream on," she muttered to herself.

"I caught that," he said with a smile, "and I do."

"James, you're right. I am in a fantastic mood and I'm not going to allow you to spoil it. How's that?"

"I'm not sure how to take that."

"Hmmm. I think you're taking it the way I meant it."

"Oh so the ice queen is beginning to thaw. Miracles do happen. Anyway, my lovely, hurry on your way to makeup and wardrobe because we are about to be called to set. Also, I would encourage you to be on your best behavior today because I have it on good authority that Nigel is not in a very good mood."

Alexandra laughed out loud. "I'm sorry, but is he ever in a good mood? If he is I've missed it."

"One thing you have to remember, Miss Martel, is that Nigel is a genius and when you find genius you accept how it shows up. I'll tell you something else. Nigel can make or break your career. It is a privilege for you, for all of us, to be working with him. I've seen him turn more than one unimaginative script into a masterpiece, so I'd lose the pettiness, my dear."

She turned to face him. "James, not even one of your routine slap downs is going to destroy my good mood today, so stop stroking. I know very well Nigel is a genius. I'd be the first to say so and I do feel enormously privileged to be given the opportunity to work with him. So if I agree he's not in a good mood, it's just that. He's in a sour mood. I am in no way questioning his brilliance as a director. Actually, I am in awe of the man."

"You know what, Alexandra? You're a witch but that's not the way you spell it."

She laughed, unexpectedly enjoying this morning's sparring match. "And since we're being childish, Mr. Langford, you're a brick, only that's not the way…. Oh never mind. I'm not getting caught up in this game with you. We have another kissing scene today so I'm hoping you've left the garlic alone."

"Don't give me any ideas. One thing I will say for you, Alexandra, you have managed to stay in character this whole time. You're a wonderful method actress, completely inhabiting the character of Sari

Patton. You're exactly the way she is, impossible."

"And to you, James, I say ditto."

She laughed as she started over to the makeup trailer, falling into step with Candace Wilmer who was cast as the Pattons' devious maid.

Ignoring the maid, James glared at her, although she was sure she saw a twinkle in his eye. James was who he was, perhaps not so bad once you got to know him. She wished he'd stop those ridiculous come-ons. Perhaps it was all part of his ego trip, and he was not interested in her at all. Saints be praised if that was the case.

* * *

The man couldn't believe it! Even after all his careful planning he'd missed his one golden opportunity to snatch Miss Alexandra Martel. He himself was never up and about earlier than eight o'clock in the morning, an inveterate night owl. But since he hadn't been able to sleep much last night, not with the noose tightening around his neck, he'd decided to take a drive by the movie location at daybreak. And who does he see running merrily along the side of the road? Why one starlet ripe for the picking, that's who.

But she'd been talking to someone in a pick-up truck and so he hadn't been able to make his move. That irked him to no end. Nevertheless he now had a valuable piece of information in his arsenal. He'd accidently cottoned on to when she was most vulnerable. Talk about low hanging fruit. It would never get much easier than that, alone on the road in the early morning when there was practically no traffic at all.

He'd hurried and made the turn once he saw the pick-up go on his way, but by the time he'd returned she'd already gone into that trailer compound. He was getting closer, and there was always tomorrow with its sunny forecast. She would for sure be out running in the morning and then he'd have her. He already felt some of the tension begin to ease out of his rock hard muscles. Plan A was about to be put into action. Possibly he'd get to live after all.

Pulling off the road at a provincial picnic site he double checked to make sure he had everything he needed; chloroform, rope, duct tape, hood, and a big ole' tarp to cover her up once he had her in the back of his SUV. He was practically salivating now that his moment of relief was almost at hand, but it was all about the money.

* * *

In one sense the day seemed to drag by agonizingly slow for Alexandra, although she had to put all of that in the back of her mind to concentrate on her work. James was right, Nigel was especially nitpicky today, but she managed to shine in whatever he asked of her. Even the kiss was tolerable, which made her wonder if perhaps she hadn't been the problem all along. She imagined she was kissing Beau and let it flow from there. She knew James felt her response and really got into it, which clearly delighted Nigel. The problem was that James took encouragement from it. He had to be the most persistent person on the face of the earth. He couldn't contemplate that every woman didn't want him. It was purely a matter of time before he brought them around to his way of thinking.

"Alexandra," he breathed against her ear when "CUT" was clearly heard by all and sundry. "You turned me on."

She puffed a sigh. "Down boy, it's called acting."

He was all calf eyes. "Acting will only take you so far, darlin'. I know a visceral response when I see it, or should I say feel it. You want me, admit it."

She chuckled. "James, you know you're a drop dead gorgeous man. I don't need to tell you that."

"Yes you do, because I never get tired of hearing it. And I don't think I've ever heard it from you."

"Okay then, there it is, but don't let it go to your head." She thought in that moment she'd never uttered a more ridiculous statement, but what the heck. She was in a fabulous mood.

"I'm going to put that away in my heart."

"You put it anywhere you want, James. I'm not telling you something you've never heard before, but again, for the record, I'm not interested in anything more than a professional relationship with you."

"You like to play hard to get is all, but I have enough patience for both of us. One day you'll thank me for this, you wait and see."

"Okay. Whatever you say."

"One thing is for certain right now, Alexandra. You made Nigel a very happy director today. I have never seen his mood *improve*, it's usually the other way around. You know, my dear," he said, pausing to look at her meaningfully, "he gets lonely too."

She gaped at him, her face turning to stone. "I'm going to pretend I never heard that."

"What! I didn't say...."

"No, you didn't, but you were insinuating, and you can stop it right now. I happen to know that Mr. Garretson is a married man and even if he wasn't I wouldn't be interested. And besides, since we're talking about hookups, aren't you and that production assistant counting sheep together? Isn't one enough? Why are you still hounding me?"

He shook his head. "You are naïve, Alexandra. That might be part of your charm, but I'm never quite sure."

She shrugged. "Be that as it may, I like the me I am just fine."

* * *

The rest of the day went surprisingly well, despite James' constant haranguing. He'd hinted he might be interested in recommending her to star with him in his next movie, but she'd not been approached, and filming was scheduled to start in the next couple of months. Retribution would certainly help send her on her way, Twice Dead might turn her into a bankable star. Knowing the actor it could be all talk. You never knew with James and the thought of putting up with him for another two or three months on top of this gave her considerable pause, no matter what the prize might be.

She glanced at her watch. Only a couple of hours now before Beau was supposed to call and she felt butterflies take flight in her stomach. She'd never been this excited to hear from a man. That included several years ago when a handsome co-star of hers, Henry Webster, had asked her out. She'd been over the moon but alas, Henry had turned out to be a dud. Beau held much more promise.

She thought too about her run this morning in this gorgeous Belleisle countryside. What a delicious way to start her day. She could hardly wait for morning when she'd lace up and head out again.

Chapter 11

Alexandra was stepping out of the shower when she heard her cellphone ringing. It was seven o'clock but perhaps Beau had decided to call her earlier than planned. Okay, no problem.

"Hi, darling! How is my little movie star?" came Grandmother Bridger's unmistakable voice. "I haven't heard from you in a while, and I was wondering if everything was all right way up there in Belleisle. I got your birthday arrangement and thank you very much for that. It was absolutely lovely, and the bottle of pink champagne was a nice touch. My granddaughters are so thoughtful. I'll save the bubbly for when my friends come over to play cards."

"I'm glad you liked my gift," said Alexandra, thrilled to receive a call from her grandmother. "It's wonderful to hear your voice!"

Next to Ginger she was the closest of the three girls to their one grandparent. Not that Gram didn't adore Naomi too, all three were loved unconditionally. There might be some conditions from time to time when it came to earning her affection, but all was usually positively resolved.

"Are they keeping you busy?" Gram wanted to know.

"It's always super busy around here. It can be intense for the weeks you're on location, and then it's all over except for a few post-production things, and promotion. The actors are expected to actively participate in promoting the film. It's always in everyone's best interests to have a motion picture do well at the box office."

"How are you holding up? It must get tiring after a while. I don't know how you do it myself. If I was having a bad day I couldn't pretend otherwise. I don't think acting would be for me."

Alexandra thought about Nigel Garretson trying to direct Gram to do something she had decided for whatever reason she didn't want to do. It would be an epic showdown. Grandmother Bridger was every bit as fiery as Nigel, so there'd be no shortage of excitement.

"It's not easy at times. I will admit that, but you do what you're supposed to do anyway. You could say that about anything in life I guess. Good with the bad."

"And I suppose they're on such a tight schedule everyone has to be on their best behavior. No, I don't think moviemaking would be for me."

Alexandra laughed. "I don't know about best behavior, but like the old adage says, the show must go on. You have to forget who you are and what your problems are and become who you're supposed to be for those few minutes or few hours, whatever the case may be."

"My hat's off to you. I was saying the other day I always knew you'd do something with acting."

"You mean because of all that school stuff I was involved in? I don't think there was a play or a musical I didn't manage to get myself cast in. They couldn't get rid of me."

"You're a born actress, Alexandra. You were always putting on what you called funny shows at home when you were a kid, roping your sisters into getting up on stage with you. You've got a good healthy sense of drama about you."

"Thank you, I think."

"I mean it in a positive way, but I do want to talk to you about something very important concerning your work. Do you have to compromise yourself in any way to get the job done? That's what worries me."

"Compromise myself to get the job done?"

"I think you know what I mean, Alexandra. What I'm asking is do you have to take your clothes off in that movie?"

Surely Ginger hadn't said anything about her nude scene in Retribution. Both she and Naomi had promised they wouldn't. But how else would Gram know if one of them hadn't let it slip.

"Ahhhh...."

"I take that to be a yes. So do I understand the situation correctly? Will you be half-dressed at some point?"

She'd been dreading a confrontation like this because their grandmother was such a dedicated surrogate mother. She realized now she had foolishly believed it would not be an issue. Gram wasn't a moviegoer in any sense of the word, so she wouldn't ever have to know about it. She supported Alexandra one hundred percent and never missed one of her television appearances but didn't care to watch movies. "I'd sooner read a good book instead," she'd always said, and Alexandra had not taken offence.

"Yes, Gram, I will be taking my clothes off," she said after a moment, throwing caution to the wind. In for a penny in for a pound. "To be honest I'll be as naked as the day I was born."

There was silence on the other end of the line, plenty of it. In fact she began to wonder if she'd lost the connection when her grandmother spoke again.

"Alexandra, I forbid you to do such a thing! You do not need to take your clothes off in public in order to be a success in life. I will not allow you to cheapen yourself."

"Gram, it's only a movie and it's what the script calls for."

"What the script calls for! Would you have sex with a man on camera if that's what the script called for?"

Now the silence was on Alexandra's end.

"Oh dear lord! Alexandra! Do not tell me you intend to do that too!"

"It's not real, Gram. It's just made to look real."

"It's the same thing, young lady. It's equally as bad! Everyone will think you did it because that's how it's meant to look."

"It's movie magic," she said in defense of her actions and knew as soon as her ill-chosen words were out of her mouth there would be an explosion. And there was, of monumental proportions.

“Magic! It’s pornography!”

“Thank you very much for thinking I’d do such a thing. This is a regular movie scene.”

“About a man and a woman rolling around in bed together naked. Have I got that part right?”

“That’s what will be happening, but it’ll be a closed set. There’ll be myself and another actor, the director and technical people.”

“So you’ll only be doing it in front of about a dozen people. How wonderful for them. What about the thousands of people who’ll see such a spectacle when the movie goes into theatres? Hmmm?”

“Gram…”

“I’m forbidding you to do it, Alexandra! I am serious, I forbid it!”

“I have to do it.”

“You don’t *have* to do anything. You were taught at a very young age to stand up for yourself and say no when the situation called for it. It’s as simple as that.”

“It’s not simple at all, Gram. I’m under contract. I’m obligated to do it.”

“Why did you sign such a contract then? Have you taken leave of your senses?”

"Gram, I've worked hard to get where I am in this industry, you know that. It's one little bedroom scene for heaven's sake. Please don't get yourself all upset over nothing."

She was dreading that *one little bedroom scene* with everything in her, but Nigel was one of those directors who refused to use body doubles. Authenticity was Nigel's personal banner of excellence, and he would not budge an inch.

"Alexandra, I want you to tell that director of yours you can't do this thing. Please, dear. You have to listen to reason. You can't be naked in public!"

"If it helps any I'll be working with an intimacy coach."

"A coach!" she sputtered. "I've heard everything now."

Alexandra sighed. "Sorry, I guess intimacy coordinator is the more accurate term. These scenes are very technical, Gram, and take a lot of preparation. An intimacy coordinator is part of the overall team. I'll admit I'm nervous about doing the scene, so the intimacy coordinator is trying to help me become more comfortable with it."

"Don't get too comfortable with it for heavens sake, you'll be making a habit of it."

"I know it's hard to understand all of this stuff, Gram, but the end goal for everyone is to make the movie the best it can be. The director and I have already discussed the whole thing. He's walked me through exactly what will happen. It's a nude scene, but they have things in place for when...."

"Things such as what, pray tell?" her grandmother demanded, cutting her off.

"Gram...."

"Alexandra, I'm clearly over eighteen. Tell me."

"Okay, for one thing James will be wearing a modesty pouch and I'll also have a genital guard."

There was a loud moan on the other end of the connection. "I am so sorry I asked. I don't want to hear anymore because I am getting the message loud and clear that it makes no difference whatsoever how I feel about it. You're going to go ahead with it, and if that's the case let me tell you how disappointed I am that you would do such a thing. I am so glad your dear mother is not alive right now to know about it. Her own daughter flopping around on a bed, genital guard or not, with some man she's just met. Never in my life have I ever heard of a more shameful thing. You were raised better than that, Alexandra. You were raised to be a lady, but you're stubborn. More stubborn than your sisters I will have to say, and that's going some."

"Gram, a few minutes ago you were telling me how proud you were of me."

"That was before you told me about that! *That* is a very big deal to me. My granddaughter cavorting naked with some stranger in a pouch!"

Alexandra was suppressing laughter at Gram's comical outrage. But she knew her grandmother was serious and so she had to do what she could to reassure her. "I know, Gram. Honestly, I'm not looking forward to it either, but this movie was such a big break for me and it was a chance to star with James Langford."

There was a long pause. "James Langford? I know who he is. I saw him on a television entertainment show last week. He's in this movie you're making right now. I can't remember when I've ever seen such a handsome man. With that blonde hair of his and those blue eyes he'd melt a woman's heart. A mighty good-looking man if you want my opinion. That's who you'll be having sex with?"

"Pretend sex, Gram."

"Right, pretend sex. So you say that James Langford is involved?"

She withheld the fact she thought of James Langford as a woman-hungry narcissist.

"He's the one."

"Hmmm. He's the one you're going to be doing that awful scene with."

"Again, he's the one."

"I wonder, is he as reluctant as you are about doing this?"

"I would say he's not reluctant at all."

"I'll bet he's not reluctant. Not much wonder these men like to be movie stars. But James Langford. Oh, Alexandra, you didn't mention it was him."

If she didn't miss her guess entirely, that had changed the water on the beans.

"Gram, what we're talking about is the nuts and bolts of making a movie. That's all. Everything will be very tastefully shown on the screen. I'll have to go through something I'm not entirely comfortable with, but I'm not going to be taken advantage of or exploited. Nigel Garretson is an award-winning director and at the end of the day the movie will be good. So I know you're upset about this, and I can understand that, but let me tell you something important. I promise you this will be the first and last nude scene I ever do. I am sorry I agreed to it, and I won't ever do another one. It's not in my wheelhouse. Does that help?"

"It does help," her grandmother agreed, miraculously mollified, no doubt still thinking about the fact her granddaughter was working with James Langford. He *was* a pretty big deal in Hollywood.

"And also know if there was any way out of doing this, I'd take it, believe me. But I don't want to be sued into the Stone Age because that's what would happen or get fired and never be hired again. I have to set my teeth to it and get it done."

"Okay, Alexandra. I suppose you're right. I don't like it at all, but I do understand. I'll try not to think about it."

She breathed a huge sigh of relief. She was not afraid to do battle with her grandmother. She didn't care for it, but backing down wasn't an option either and she believed Gram respected her for that.

"Alexandra, I don't know if I ever told you this, but of the three of you, you are the most like your mother."

Now she hadn't expected her grandmother to say that. She remembered her mother to be feisty, and a fighter. Tragically she hadn't been able to win her fight against the deadliest battle of all, cancer. She was sure her loss would always resonate with all four of them. She missed her mother every day. In fact if she were in a scene that called for tears, she never had to drill down very deep. If she thought about her mother they were always there in ample supply.

"I consider that a compliment. Thank you."

"A compliment, yes, in many ways, but of the three of you, you're the most headstrong. I begged her not to marry your father, that loser, but she went ahead with it anyway and look how that turned out. Nothing would change her mind and she suffered greatly because of it. I'm praying that's not the case with you too, Alexandra. I am relieved you've given me your assurance about not doing such things in the future. No amount of money is worth that, darling."

She had to smile. Gram made it sound as though she'd be parading around naked in front of everyone, but she let it go. If Gram was settling down on the subject, then best to leave sleeping dogs lie.

She glanced at the clock. Seven minutes to eight and Beau would be calling soon, but she wanted to leave Gram on a positive note.

"Gram I do have what might be good news to share with you. I say what might be because it's so new, but let's say I'm hopeful."

"Okay then, dear, spit it out. Tell me James Langford has asked you to marry him and I will die a happy woman."

She didn't see that one coming. *She* would die a happy woman if she never had to see James Langford again. How about that! Why had she opened her big mouth? Now she'd have to disappoint her grandmother all over again. It would be very unprofessional to badmouth a fellow cast member, and especially in this case to ruin Gram's hero image of the man.

"To be honest, he has talked about that, but...."

"Grab him, Alexandra! You're never going to do any better than that in the man department."

"Gram, I won't be grabbing him because he, well, grabs anything he can get if you know what I mean. I agree with you he's very handsome and a great actor but trust me, you don't want me married to him. *I* don't want me married to him."

"Oh, Alexandra. What am I going to do with you, dear? I'm beginning to wonder if you have any aspirations to marry at all, to have children. A career is wonderful, and I applaud you for what you have accomplished so far. I'm very proud of you."

"I hear a but coming, Gram."

"But I don't want to see you miss out on the opportunity to fall in love, get married to someone who will love you, be a good partner and give you children."

She smiled. "I want all that too, Gram. Now I hate to cut this conversation short, but I *have* met someone. We want to get to know each other and that's about to start happening soon. Like in about a minute because he's supposed to call me at eight."

"My goodness! I'll let you go, but not before you promise to give me a full report."

She couldn't help but laugh. Gram missed an ideal career when she didn't join the military. She was officer material if ever anyone was. The command was always in her voice, but no matter what the message might be, it always came from a place of love.

* * *

As soon as she got off the phone she began to towel-dry her hair, which meant it had more than its share of waves since she didn't have a chance to use a blow dryer. It had been a difficult conversation at times tonight, but that didn't matter as much as knowing someday there would be no more talks like that with Gram. It would happen all too soon she feared considering her grandmother's age. She pushed the depressing thought from her mind. It was too upsetting to even contemplate.

She thought of her lines she had to look over again in preparation for tomorrow, but she'd do that first thing in the morning instead. Born with an ability to memorize quickly, she already had the part of Sari Patton down to a tee, but she left nothing to chance. She had to be completely in the zone when she was called to set because Nigel would accept nothing less.

The upcoming nude scene flashed through her mind. It was one thing to act, call on emotions. It was quite another to get to where she needed to be with James to do the bedroom scene.

Next time she'd ask her agent to try for a romantic comedy. She wasn't aware she possessed any particular comedic skills, but it could be an untapped talent. One never knew until they tried. She did enjoy drama though, seemed more naturally inclined toward it so Gram was right all along. It appeared she knew her granddaughters better than they knew themselves sometimes.

Alexandra remembered what she'd been like as a child. She'd always been a girly girl, more so than Ginger or Naomi. Of the three girls, she was the one who liked dressing up and painting her nails. She remembered the time she'd gotten into her mother's makeup. It could very well have been the ruined carpet that made her mother so angry.

Anyway, she never tried it again, but Gram had understood and bought her a toy makeup kit. Hey, she should have thought to mention that when they were talking. Tell her, in jest, she was responsible for all this theatrical stuff. Gram would have gotten a laugh out of that.

At exactly eight o'clock her cellphone rang, and the caller was identified as B. Remington. Her heart did a somersault as she pressed TALK and settled into an armchair in the living room.

"Hi, this is Beau," he said after her hello, and she appreciated the deep rich timbre of his voice. "Are you still able to talk or has something come up?"

See? Thoughtful right out of the gate "No, everything is cool and I'm able to talk. So how was your day?"

He groaned which meant he must have had a bad one. "It's been eventful," he answered her honestly. "When I saw you this morning I was on my way home to take a shower."

She hesitated. "You were up all night with a sick animal?" she guessed.

"No, sick people you might say," and told her about sending inspectors to a farm and what they found. "So they roughed me up a bit at first, that's where I got the black eye in case you were wondering. Last night they set fire to my clinic."

"Beau! That's horrible! Is it a complete loss?"

"No, thankfully only the back end was destroyed. We've got a good volunteer fire department here and the members live close by. They had it out in no time flat. We're in the middle of sorting out the overall damage, like from smoke and water. Anyway, it could have been worse. So how did your day go?"

"Okay I guess."

"You sound hesitant."

She sighed. "How would you like to have to kiss James Langford?"

He laughed and it was a warm, sexy sound that gave her goose bumps. She sensed he didn't do it often. "No, I wouldn't want to kiss James Langford, but that's just me. Why, is he not a good kisser?"

She was laughing now too. "Forget I said that. It's not very nice to kiss and tell. Besides, it was a movie kiss so it doesn't count."

He laughed with her. "I'm not sure what the difference is, but that's okay. I guess you do what you have to do."

She explained a movie kiss to him, the placement of hands by both actors. She knew as she was doing so that James did not respect those professional boundaries. Anyway, that information wouldn't do Beau any good so she'd keep it to herself.

"I Googled you, Alexandra," he said, thankfully changing the subject. "I've seen some of the things you've been in. You're good."

She flushed with pleasure. "Thank you."

"So what's the end game here? You want to be a major motion picture star? Not that you're not already a star," he added quickly.

She thought for a moment. What an unusual question, although not an unreasonable one. It was nice he was showing interest in her work and not dismissing it to talk about himself like a lot of guys would. He seemed genuinely interested and she liked that about him already.

She laughed, giddily nervous that she was actually talking to him because he had quickly become so important to her. On the other hand his relaxed manner put her completely at ease.

"I certainly don't think of myself as a star," she explained. "I'm a movie personality. I like to act. Retribution is my biggest project yet and I'm hoping it will help establish me in the industry. There's such fierce competition that succeeding is about twenty-five percent talent. There are a lot of talented out of work actors out there on any given day. It's also twenty-five percent timing, and fifty percent good luck in my opinion. I was fortunate to get cast in this movie because the original lead had to back out. At least that's what I was told, but since I'd already tested for the part, I was signed. James is a friend of the director and he spoke for me so here I am, Sari Patton."

"I could never do what you do."

That was the second time she'd heard that within the last hour. "It's honestly not that hard. Memorize your lines and say them."

He chuckled. "There's a little bit more to it than that I think. There's that very important thing called talent and you either have it or you don't. I wouldn't call myself a movie buff, no offence, but I've seen enough to know that without talent a pretty face is just a pretty face, no matter who's wearing it. I was reading the other day about this guy who was considered to be the next big thing. I mean he had everything they'd look for in terms of appearance, but he couldn't act, at least not very well. So he was basically finished before he even started. I think that's sad because from what I read he was a very nice guy."

"It is sad, and the entertainment industry has a lot of casualties, for sure. That's why I feel so lucky. It's not an easy job by any stretch of the imagination, but the money and benefits are great. There's a study supposedly done of millions of actors dating back to the 1800's. It said the unemployment rate for actors is something like ninety percent and two percent were making a living at it. Anyway, I'm curious about *your* work. You're a veterinarian? A veterinarian surgeon?"

"I am a veterinary surgeon, but I do much more than surgery. I do the regular veterinary work too. I guess you could call me a mixed practice veterinarian because I work with both large and small animals. That means horses, cows and other livestock, but also your run of the mill dogs, cats, rabbits, that kind of thing."

"I'm impressed, I truly am. It must have taken you a lot of years to become a vet and a surgeon on top of that."

"About nine years altogether, give or take, but the education never ends. There are always medical advancements, changing client's needs and everything across the board to do with veterinary medicine in general. It's the same with any career. I love to learn so I guess that takes care of that."

"Fascinating. I love animals too."

"Do you? I like to hear that. Any preferences?"

"I love horses. I've always wanted to learn how to ride properly but I live in Toronto and my work more or less keeps me in the city. None of my roles so far have required me to ride but I've always thought I should learn in case something like that comes up."

"I have three horses. One old, one not so old, and an eight year-old."

"That sounds wonderful, Beau. A man who loves animals is usually a nice guy in my opinion. What are the names of your horses?"

"Chance."

"Which one is Chance?"

He chuckled. "They all are. One is a rescue and I have two surrenders, and they're all named Chance. So since that's the name they know, that's what I kept. If you ever get any time off I'd like to take you riding. I'd put you on Chance number one because he's older and very quiet."

"That sounds like so much fun," she said with a sigh, "but I work a six day week and I usually use my day off to get rested up."

"Your schedule sounds like my schedule," he laughed.

"This could be complicated then," she said, chuckling. "We're supposed to wrap up sometime around the end of August, and I'll have more free time then, but that depends on if we keep to schedule. Our director is very good in that regard because to go over the allotted time usually means going over budget. A lot of movies do that, a little or a lot, but for Nigel that's a big no no. He brings his movies in on budget. So yes, it'll be about the end of August before I'm finished here, but maybe sooner."

He was quiet for a moment, and she worried he'd immediately lose interest because of her unavailability. She would love nothing better than to go out on a date with him, supposing that's what he had in mind. Go for that horseback ride.

"I'm guessing that day off would be Sunday. If so I want to book you now. Will that work?"

She was about to agree when she remembered she'd promised her assistant Pam she'd go with her to see the famous Hopewell Rocks on Sunday. That was their only available time, and the Sunday after that it was off with her to the Reversing Falls. Pam was from Toronto and fascinated with the ocean, so she was trying to see some of New Brunswick's seaside phenomena while she was in the province. Alexandra had promised those trips to her before she'd ever met Beau, and it wouldn't be right to cancel.

"You're right, it is Sunday, but unfortunately I'm tied up for the next two Sundays."

"So that means it'll be three weeks before we can get together."

He didn't sound upset, but how much fun would it be to try to get close to someone with her kind of schedule? Not much she'd guess. Hers was not a normal life. If she got the part in Twice Dead she'd be gone for months on location in California. She couldn't imagine starting a new relationship under those circumstances so would it be fairer to Beau to back off now? It wouldn't work if she had to routinely disappoint him and that's what it could amount to over time. She felt uncharacteristically frustrated, sad.

"Beau," she began, a slight tremble in her voice, "if you want to hang up right now and forget this whole thing, I'll understand."

Chapter 12

"Whoa! Where did that come from?" he asked, surprised.

"It's just that you'd like to take me out, that I'd like to go out with you, but I can't, not for a while. So I think if you...."

"Alexandra, I can think for myself," he told her without sugar coating. "You don't need to do it for me. I want to take you out and I'm thrilled you'd like to go out with me, but I completely understand your circumstances. I'm very busy right now anyway what with the clinic being damaged and all. My schedule is crazy, so believe me I understand. Yours is a unique situation, but surely we can fit something in along the way until you're done with the movie. Until then we can talk to each other on the phone. Grab a few seconds here and there when you're jogging or something. You wouldn't happen to be going out for a run tomorrow morning would you?"

She groaned. "No, I was thinking about it because I enjoyed it so much this morning, but we have a super early call tomorrow. Besides Nigel would freak if he knew I was going out like that, alone. He seems to think I should have a security detail with me like I'm some big deal star or a member of the Royal family, and I'm neither."

"He's being protective, and I can understand that. You don't know how someone would react if they recognized you."

"One good thing about being here in Belleisle is everyone is friendly and nice, a lovely little community in the country. I don't think you'll find too many creeps around."

He thought about the Ratchett brothers. There were creeps here all right and you apparently didn't have to beat the bushes very hard to find them. All he had to do was look at his black eye to be reminded of that. He thought too about the animals that had suffered at the hands of those abusive brothers. Some people should not be allowed to own animals.

"You're right to an extent I guess," he agreed, trying not to be unreasonable. "I couldn't believe it the other day when you said you were from New Brunswick. I mean what are the odds. I thought sure you were from LA or something and up here doing the movie.”

“I love it here in New Brunswick, but I could hardly wait to get to Toronto when I finished school because that’s where Canada’s film and television capital is, Hollywood North. I live there because of the entertainment industry, but my heart will always be in this province. Toronto is nice though, it’s a great city.”

“I agree with you, it is. I’ve spent a lot of time in Toronto.”

“You’re kidding!” she exclaimed, surprised. “Is that where you went to school by any chance?”

“Yes it was. I graduated from the University of Guelph, which isn’t too far away. So it seems we have one more thing in common.”

“But you were born in New Brunswick too?”

“Born in New Brunswick and raised on a horse ranch in Jemseg. You’d love it there, Alexandra. My Mum and Dad still run it and it’s stocked with quarter horses.”

“It sounds so wonderful,” she said dreamily. “Wouldn’t it be nice if I could be in a movie on a place like that with horses, dogs and everything. That would be so much fun.”

"Or star in your own real-life movie," he said with a smile in his voice. "Live on one instead of pretending to live on one."

"Hmmm," she mused. "That would be a leap. Someday I could have a ranch of my own and raise horses. Now wouldn't that be something. They say anything's possible if you set your mind to it."

He laughed. "I think there needs to be more than one of you to do all the things you want to do with your life."

She laughed too. "Actually, there is more than one of me."

"Oh? You've managed to clone yourself have you?"

"In a manner of speaking, yes. Or should I say nature did it for us. I'm a triplet, Beau. That's not part of my bio because I try to keep my personal life, personal, as much as I can anyway."

"Go away! You're a triplet?"

"I'm serious. My sisters are Naomi and Ginger. We're identical and we even still wear our hair the same way. Ginger started cutting hers short a few years ago but her husband likes it long. Now we all three have long hair, and of course everything else is the same."

"I don't believe what I'm hearing. Alexandra, you're so beautiful it's hard to get my head around the fact there's two more the very same. So why hasn't Hollywood snapped up all three of you?"

She settled deeper into the armchair and drew her feet up under her. "Because I'm the only one interested in acting, and I'm not the first multiple who has ever been in motion pictures. There are others too, it's just not well known."

"What do your sisters do?"

"Naomi is a computer programmer, and Ginger is a writer. She's also an office manager, but she's won awards for her writing. So I guess she's creative too. Naomi is married to a rancher, Hayden Barlowe down in Bloomfield and they're expecting their first child in a few months. It's going to be a boy, and Ginger is married to Shane Elliott, a police officer and hostage negotiator. They have one little girl, Heather, named after our mother."

"I'm gobsmacked. You're a triplet. I guess with two of the three already taken I was lucky to meet the one who's still available. I'm kidding! I know each of you is your own person. I don't care if you're a quintuplet or a singlet, I wanted to meet you and I'm glad I did. Have you ever been married, Alexandra?"

"Not even close. I have been one hundred percent committed to my career, but as Gram keeps telling me I've got to make room in my life for more. She won't rest until all three of us are married and have children."

"I have a question for you. We were talking about James Langford last time when we got interrupted. I believe you told me you're not engaged to him."

"That's right. I'm not."

"Okay, because he told me there was going to be a wedding, and I believe he meant you'd be his bride."

She let out a long sigh. "I don't know why he does stuff like that. I wonder sometimes if it's his warped sense of humour. I don't know."

"I don't think he was kidding when he warned me away from you, but if it helps I didn't take him seriously. Still, I had to ask to make sure. Don't need to be stepping in somewhere when I'm not wanted."

"I'm glad you asked again so there won't be any misunderstanding. I'm not engaged to anyone, much to the consternation of my grandmother. She's more or less made it her mission in life to get us all to the altar. Our mother died quite young from cancer and so my grandmother, Mum's mother, took it upon herself to be there for us more or less as a surrogate mother. Believe me, she takes that commitment very seriously. She's in her nineties now."

"And frail I would imagine."

"Frail! Grandmother Bridger? Tropical Storm Bridger would be a better name. Gram does things her way and she takes no prisoners. You fetch up against her and you won't soon forget about it. I was talking to her earlier this evening and she was getting after me about the nude scene I've got coming up, a bedroom scene with James Langford. She was not happy about it, and she only backed off when she realized it was *the* James Langford I'd be doing it with. She's not into movie stars, but she adores him for some reason."

There was an understandable pause on the other end of the line. "How do you feel about doing that?" he asked, hesitance in his voice.

"What, about Gram being a force to be reckoned with, or her liking James Langford?"

"Very funny. Neither. I'm wondering how you feel about doing nude bedroom scenes?"

"With James Langford?"

"With anyone."

Oh no, he wasn't going to be a chest beating alpha male was he. He was definitely an alpha male, but he didn't seem on first impression to be the possessive type. Still, one never knew. On the other hand, even though they'd just met he naturally wouldn't like her taking off her clothes in front of another man. Participating in a sex scene with said man. That went with the territory. That would be the reaction of any partner, potential or otherwise.

"Honestly? I basically talked myself into it and I thought I'd be all right once I got used to the idea. But the truth is, I'm dreading it like you wouldn't believe. And before you tell me to refuse to do it, like Gram did, I'm under contract. A contract I signed saying I would be okay with it. I knew the situation from the start and agreed to it once I talked it over with the director. Now I'm stuck, but I have to get it done. That's all there is to it. It's going to be a closed set, but there'll be people in the room, including James."

"Who will be practically salivating I would imagine."

"As like as not knowing him, but there it is. I can tell you one thing. It's my first and last motion picture nude scene. Period. Now can we please move on to something else? I'm sorry, Beau, I don't want to talk about it. Actors and actresses do that kind of stuff every day and get through it, so I will too. And the director will do all he can to make me comfortable with it. I know he will. Nigel is Nigel, but he's not a bad guy when it comes to stuff like this."

"Okay, nuff said."

"Beau...."

"Yes?"

"Have you ever been married? Do you have children?"

"No to both. I came close to getting married once but realized it would have been to the wrong person and got out of it. Anyway, as much as I'm enjoying talking to you, I've got to let you go. I haven't had any real sleep since night before last and I've got a crazy day coming up tomorrow. I need to get my beauty sleep."

"Me too."

He chuckled. "I've seen you, remember? You don't need beauty sleep but is it okay if I give you a call tomorrow night, same time?"

Alexandra felt the smile build all the way up from her toes and land comfortably on her face. "I'd like that, Beau. Goodnight."

* * *

The man made sure he was in the area at five o'clock the next morning, all supplies on hand but despite the fact that he cruised the route where he'd seen Alexandra running, there was no sign of her. He'd even parked on a side road back far enough under some trees so as not to be easily detected, but she had not passed by. He couldn't believe his poor luck. Most joggers were out every day weren't they? Not every once in a while. She must be the exception.

He smoked his last cigarette down to the filter, before angrily throwing the thing out the window. He should be careful not to start a forest fire, but he was irritated enough to burn the whole place down around their ears. That would mean the movie people would vacate the premises, move out in mass exodus and you could bet your sweet life she'd be one of the first to go, under armed escort likely. They knew when they had a winner, and she would be protected at all costs. That's why he'd come to understand over these past days she would not be easy to take. He couldn't believe his eyes when he'd seen her out alone with her sneakers. It might be a one-time thing.

No, he couldn't tell himself that. He had to hang in there, cover the place every morning from about four-thirty on, when it first began to get light. He knew in his heart she'd be back and when she was, he'd have her. Then his troubles would be over.

He got out of the car and made sure the cigarette butt was out cold.

* * *

Beau slept like a log that night and woke to his hand being licked by Carley, his canine alarm clock. She had the best bladder of the bunch but even that needed to be serviced on time.

After letting the dogs out he crawled back into bed for a few more minutes he told himself, but he didn't open his eyes again until over an hour later. Now he seriously did have to get up and get on with things. The horses, used to an early dose of fresh air and sunshine during the summer months, were ready to leave the barn behind for the day. He could hear old Chance pawing in his stall all the way up at the house. The black was impatient when it came to having his way, but he couldn't blame him. Not after what he'd been through, abandoned by his original owner. How anyone could turn their back on an animal was beyond him. He didn't know how people like that could sleep at night. Offering them protection and care was one of his biggest joys in life. It was one of the reasons he was so happy to get up in the morning, and he loved to share that joy with his like-minded staff at the clinic. Each and every one of them was chosen by him for their dedication to animals, and they made a good team.

It was with a light heart that he left for the clinic, not even trying to keep the smile off his face. Could Alexandra be the one? Not so fast, his protective inner voice warned. You're both living two different lifestyles. She is a city girl and a movie star to boot. First of all she wasn't available, even now, to pursue a relationship. At least they planned to keep in touch by phone. But was that the way it would always be? Him waiting for her to come home from some movie location or another. And she lived in Toronto. He lived in Belleisle and ran a veterinary clinic. They'd be like two ships passing in the night. Still, he was mightily attracted to her, and she seemed like a nice enough person. He knew in his heart this was no passing fancy. He could get serious about this girl, wanted to get serious about her if his gut was anything to go by. She was a keeper. He thought about the love scene she'd mentioned. Now that could be somewhat of a hurtle for him to get past. Then again she'd said it would be her last. That she was uncomfortable doing it. Those were all good signs as far as he was concerned. He wanted to give this a shot, somehow.

Pulling up to the clinic he saw that old faithful, Dr. Jen, was already onsite and no doubt hard at work inside. Now there was a woman any man would be lucky to find. And here she had thrown herself at him and he'd turned her down. At the end of the day though a person had to go with their heart. He knew he'd always have a good friend in her.

Hailey Cruickshank and the others pulled in behind him and now all staff was on the premises, so he suggested they assemble for a meeting.

"Okay, people," he said when everyone was gathered around. "I spoke with the claims department before I left the house, and it looks like things aren't as bad as they appeared to be right after the fire. I've got men coming any minute now to tear down what was burned and start working on rebuilding that part of the clinic. Elmer says they should be done by the end of the week. There was actually very little water damage because the rest of the clinic was secure, so it was no worse than a bad rainstorm. The lobby area got the worst of it and that can be cleaned up. Same thing with the smoke damage."

Hailey raised her hand. "What about the furniture? Some of it doesn't look too good."

Beau nodded. "I was getting to that. I've got a restoration team coming in a few minutes. They're the experts in this kind of situation. They'll clean up all the soot and smoke, and have the furniture professionally cleaned. What they don't think can be saved will be replaced."

Dr. Jen raised her hand. "They'll wash away the soot and whatever, but how do we get rid of the smell of smoke?" she asked, sniffing the air as if to underline her concern.

Beau had anticipated her question. "They tell me their technicians use air scrubbers, hydroxyl and ozone generators and when they're done there'll be no more smoke odor. They guarantee their work. And what's in our favour is that neither of our operating rooms were damaged, none of the equipment. The stuff that got hit the hardest was our supply inventory, our office supplies, pet foods, OTC products and things like that. All of that is a complete loss so we'll have to access our full inventory list and order replacement stock. I would assume there'll be a one or two-day delivery on that so when it arrives we'll store it in the first operating room until the back end is done.

"I've been assured by the cleanup teams everything will be finished within the next few days and the good news is we should be back up and running by the first of next week. Now I'm waiting for Elmer and his crew to finish the rebuilding and like I say they promise they'll have it ready by the end of the week. So we're in good shape. And now for the good news. I don't want any of you to have sleepless nights over losing a week's pay. We all need our income so there'll be no disruption in the payroll. I appreciate all you've done so far, so after the supplies have been ordered I want you to go home while the work is being carried out here. Take a few days for yourselves and be ready to come back next Monday. Are we good?"

There were understandable smiles from everyone, and even a couple of woohoo's. No one had verbalized their concern about loss of income, but he knew everything had looked grim at the outset. Soon this would be just a bad memory.

* * *

The day was a demanding one with several scenes to be shot, but Alexandra breezed through them her heart lighter than it had been in a long while. The funny thing was people didn't realize they were lonely until someone came into their lives and filled up the hole that oftentimes they weren't even aware existed. Beau was doing that for her and oh how she longed to be able to go out on a date with him. Spend time with him face to face, rather than over the phone. Now that would be truly wonderful. She had to remind herself to slow down a little. After all they'd met once, for a few minutes. Still, her heart told her he was the one.

And now, happily, it was only two hours before he was supposed to call. So she decided to cook herself a good hearty supper with lots of steamed vegetables. She was adamant about maintaining a healthy diet and enjoyed eating good food. At seven o'clock, as if a replay of the previous evening, her telephone rang. It was Ginger.

"Hi, Sis!" Ginger said cheerfully.

Alexandra pretended to be angrier than she was. "Don't you hi Sis me, you Judas!"

"Judas! What!"

"You told Gram about me doing that nude scene and you knew I didn't want her to know."

"Oh that," said Ginger lightly. "I swear to you it came out by accident. I would never betray a confidence. I guess I did this time, didn't I? I realized what I'd said after I said it, something like she's not looking forward to doing the nude scene or something like that. She never reacted so I figured she didn't hear me or was going to let it go."

"Was going to let it go? Ha! That'll be the day. She raked me over the coals for twenty minutes. She might not have said anything to you, but she was already planning her attack. Let me guess, it was yesterday you let it slip."

"Right, yesterday afternoon."

"Okay, and she called me last night and forbid me to do it! Like I could break my contract. I tell you she really let me have it."

"I'm sorry, Alexandra. I'm usually good about keeping my mouth shut when I need to, but I forgot this time. So how did it end? Are you two still speaking?"

Alexandra laughed. "When she heard it was James Langford I'd be doing it with she backed off, if you can believe it. Turns out she thinks he's a great guy, but she's still not happy her precious granddaughter will be dropping the sheet as it were in front of him. Anyway, no problem, I let things slip sometimes too. All is forgiven."

"Good, because I've called to give you some great news."

"Dish!"

"I'm pregnant again!"

"You are not. Wow!"

"Believe me, this wasn't planned but Shane and I are happy about it. I wanted to have our children close together, and so that's what's happening. I'm already two months along I figure. So, dear sister, you're going to be an auntie again. You're going to have to get busy because Naomi and I are leaving you in the dust. Are you sure you don't want to take James Langford up on his offer? Is he still going around telling everyone you're his fiancé?"

"He does it to get my goat is what I think. I should take him up on it and watch him run for the hills. But anyway, never mind James. I've met someone."

"You met someone! When? How? All you ever do is work."

"I met him here on the movie location. He's a veterinarian they're bringing in when they use the animals in case there's an accident or something. Let me tell you, he's a definite ten, and nice to boot. As you know I'm tied up here for the next few weeks and time off is scarce, but we're talking on the phone."

"That's great, Alexandra! And then you fly back to Toronto. Does he live here?"

"Yes, he does. Please don't rain on my parade, we're getting to know each other at the moment. Nothing may come of it, but he's got my attention and he seems to like me. So we'll run with that at the moment."

"Right, don't borrow trouble. Enjoy the moment. Things have a way of working out. Look at Naomi and Hayden and their love story. For twelve years she pined for him and then he ends up getting divorced and coming back for her. Who would have ever thought it would happen? Not me! But it did and now they're happily married and expecting their first child. I guess it's true what they say, if something is meant to be, it will be. Enjoy your veterinarian. He sounds like a real catch. Ever married?"

"Nope, so we have that in common. And I like horses and he owns a ranch although he says he doesn't have the time right now to do much with it, other than to keep three horses and some dogs. He grew up on a ranch though, rides horses and all that good stuff. I'd like to see him on a horse, he is good looking I'm telling you."

"I for one am going to keep my fingers crossed it works out. In the meantime enjoy the chat. That's a good way to build a potential relationship anyway. Now, can I tell Naomi and Gram about this or am I sworn to secrecy again?"

"What good would it do?" Alexandra couldn't help needling her. "But I've already told Naomi and Gram. Now I'll say to you what I said to the others, don't make too much out of this at the moment. We haven't known each other very long and who knows how things will go. Not everything has a happy ending because we want it to. And congratulations, Ginger on baby number two. That's fantastic news."

* * *

Beau checked his watch at least a dozen times while he was doing his barn chores, then brushing the horses. It was amazing how far all three animals had come back under his care. All it took was a little work and lots of love and attention. They knew right away who loved them, and who didn't give a damn.

He looked at his watch again. The last thing he wanted was to miss his eight o'clock call to Alexandra. He knew she was on a tight schedule so he had no problem with the time deadline. She needed her sleep, so did he come to that, so it worked out best for both of them.

At eight o'clock his phone rang, and he was surprised. He was supposed to call her, but turnabout was fair play. Kinda nice, really. But when he answered the phone it was his mother on the other end.

"Beau, we think your father's had a heart attack," she told him with emotion. "The ambulance just left."

Chapter 13

"Are they taking him to Fredericton?"

"Yes, I'm headed for the car now."

"Stay where you are, Mum, I'm outta here in about two seconds. We'll take your car in case Dad can come back home, but I'll do the driving. You try to take it easy. Everything's going to be all right," he said.

He hoped he conveyed more confidence than he was feeling at the moment.

"Thank you, dear," his mother said sounding as though she was on the verge of tears. "Now don't speed and get yourself in an accident, but please come right away. I can't lose him, Beau, but I don't want to lose you either."

Promising to be careful he ended the call and headed for the back door on the trot. He could scarcely take it in. His big strong father felled by a heart attack. Impossible. But the ambulance had taken him in so they must have had good reason to suspect something was wrong. He said a silent prayer as he put the dogs into the outdoor compound. The shade house with their beds would do for the night because he wouldn't be back until morning. Everything else was taken care of.

He thought of Alexandra as he hit the main road in his pick-up for the approximately half-hour drive to his parents' Jemseg ranch. This was the way to go about it because he didn't want his mother driving while in a state of anxiety. He activated his handsfree telephone service to call Alexandra and she answered on the first ring.

"Hi, Alexandra," he said.

He loved the sound of her voice and the silent reassurance of having someone special in his life at a time like this, no matter how squeaky clean new that relationship happened to be. It felt as though he'd known her much longer than only a few days.

"Beau? Is something wrong? Your voice is different."

"Actually there is something wrong. I'm on my way to pick up my mother to go to the hospital because she thinks my father had some sort of heart attack," he said, knowing he wasn't ready to face the reality it could be a life-ending event.

"I'm so sorry to hear that! I know your mind is on that and you're trying to drive so I'm not going to keep you on the line. Please know I'm saying a prayer for him, and if it is an actual cardiac issue, that it's not too serious. When you know more I want you to call me, no matter what time of the night it is. I can't be reached tomorrow during the day unfortunately, but I'll be here around the same time tomorrow night. And Beau? I'll be saying a prayer for you and your mother too should things not go well."

He thanked her with tears in his eyes. Alexandra Martel was a keeper, their budding connection never stronger than at this moment. He'd heard it described like that when soulmates got together and judging by what he was feeling right now, it might be true.

It seemed like forever before he and his mother walked into the emergency room at the hospital in Fredericton and found someone in charge to speak with. Dr. Larkin looked much too young to be a doctor with his unruly abundance of freckles and short curly hair, but when he spoke it was with intelligence and authority.

"I'm glad to tell you your husband is going to be fine," Dr. Larkin told Beau's mother. "We've done the necessary tests and were able to determine right away he was definitely not having a heart attack. What he was experiencing were esophageal spasms, and those episodes can come on suddenly, resulting in severe chest pain. They can mimic a heart attack and a lot of people mistake them for one."

Her hand flew to her mouth, tears still not far away. "Thank God!" she said appearing weak with relief. "He was in such discomfort. We had a late supper and then he started rubbing his chest and said the pain was getting worse by the second. He explained it as a squeezing type of pain, heavy pressure, tightness. So I should not have called an ambulance?"

"You did the right thing to seek immediate medical care," he rushed to assure her. "He had to be assessed, but thankfully it was non-cardiac pain. You see the esophagus is right alongside the heart and the same sensory nerves for both organs send pain signals to the brain. It's very difficult to distinguish between the two, I mean which organ is actually causing the pain. A lot of chest pain complaints we see do turn out to be non-cardiac, but I can't stress strongly enough they still have to be investigated. In this case the news is good. He was in a lot of pain when he got here."

Beau reached to shake the doctor's hand. "I'm Beau, his son. Is he still in pain? Will the spasms pass on their own?"

The doctor finished the handshake. "We've given him some nitroglycerin and he's not in any pain now. But he will have to be seen by his family doc to check this out further. Has he had these types of spasms before do you know?"

Mrs. Remington shook her head. "This is the first I've ever heard of, but I'll make an appointment with our family doctor tomorrow."

The young doctor nodded. "Good, his GP may put him on medication to prevent it from happening again. In the meantime he's still a little shaky but raring to get back home. He's waiting for you."

Beau excused himself to make a call while his mother headed for the cubicle where her husband was waiting.

* * *

Alexandra was genuinely relieved, he could hear it in her voice when he relayed the good news about his father and explained that unfortunately there would be no telephone conversation tonight. He knew she understood his parents had been through an ordeal and were anxious to get back home, and that he planned to stay the night for their peace of mind. They chatted for a few more minutes before he saw his father walking slowly down the hall with his mother. He told her he had to go but he'd call her at the same time the following night.

* * *

When he turned out the lights that night, back in his old room, he thought about Alexandra and what it would be like to be holding her in his arms right now, with the predictable results. With a groan he rolled over onto his side. Yep, she had gotten under his skin. If he didn't know any better he'd say he was already half in love with her, no make that more than half in love with her. Call it a crush or infatuation, call it whatever you wanted, she was all he could think about. He'd have to make peace with her being held at arm's length for a while.

He remembered her early morning runs. He didn't want to interfere with her exercise routine, like some randy teenager besotted with the new girl in town. At least they'd be able to see each other for a couple of minutes now and then. Unless he missed his guess entirely he'd say she was feeling the same way about him. That didn't do much to help his present condition, especially when he thought about kissing her.

Too bad he wasn't going to be around early tomorrow morning because he'd help with chores if necessary before he headed back home. The sun rose and set on his mother and father, and he couldn't even

262

contemplate the day they would no longer be around. It was a fear he consciously worked to tamp down, because of his grandfather.

He thought of Gramp, whom he'd also idolized. His grandfather had been widowed at a relatively young age and had come to live on the family ranch when Beau was still a boy. Gramp had spent even more time with him after he retired as a family doctor, and it'd been him who'd convinced Beau to pursue his dream of becoming a veterinarian. Not everyone was a scholar, however. Beau's father wanted nothing to do with post-secondary education, happy to be a rancher. But Gramp pushed for Beau to go on to university, and he could remember to this day what he called his one caveat. Keep your own mind about things. He'd written down his thoughts on paper, and over the years Beau had committed it to memory:

"The first thing they'll hammer into you in university is to no longer take anything at face value, basically question everything in an effort to facilitate higher learning. Broaden your mind. That includes your previous belief system. In other words, treat everything with skepticism. I know I was a real pain in the butt when I was a newly minted university graduate because I was skeptical of everything. I challenged everything everyone said. I thought in terms of black and white when of course everything is *not* black and white. *That's* reality. I quickly learned that not everything *can* be explained. I learned more from my patients, most of whom were not university graduates, than I did from books. It was them who taught me, after my scientific training, how to be a good doctor. How to listen and understand and not try to come from a position of superiority because I was better educated than they were. If I didn't, how could I possibly understand them and provide proper treatment? Ask questions, yes, but also listen. Sometimes that doesn't even require a question."

Beau never forgot those words, or his grandfather's wisdom. His willingness to make room for the opinions of others, to see another side of things. Gramp told him that in his experience life was composed of grey shades with rounded corners, not sharp squares that always fit together perfectly.

His grandfather had been a positive force in his life, and he'd somehow thought, when he was much younger, that this wonderful man would live forever. But then he'd died suddenly and there'd been no chance to say good-bye. How he missed him to this day.

It was late when he finally fell asleep.

* * *

Alexandra drifted off to sleep thinking about Beau, and deeply grateful that his father was okay. Experiencing severe esophageal spasms didn't sound like much fun, but at least they weren't life threatening. She could still hear the profound relief in Beau's voice when he called her from the hospital. She'd been looking forward to a nice long chat this evening, but the fact he'd thought of her at all during a family crisis was heartwarming.

She awoke early the next morning in plenty of time to go for a nice long run. She still remembered how good it had felt the other day to get out into nature and breathe fresh air, to push her muscles in a demanding workout. The entire experience was hugely invigourating and she knew as a result she'd bring the best version of herself to set today.

Lacing on her sneakers she opted against wearing a warm-up jacket, deciding instead on a crop top and shorts. True it was brisk here in these hills in the early morning, but she warmed up fast and had been a little overdressed the other day. Pulling her long hair back in a ponytail, she stuck her sunglasses on the front panel of her baseball cap and slipped out of the compound unnoticed, except for the catering truck pulling into the yard. The driver glanced in her direction, but she put her sunglasses on and kept going.

She'd do a nice slow run today. No need to hurry she thought as she took to the road, glorying in the verdant panorama stretching out before her. Nature was a balm for the soul, why hadn't she thought to do this two weeks ago? She felt any lingering tension quickly melt away as she found her rhythm, the soles of her sneakers slapping the pavement in a satisfying pulse. In fact it felt as though her feet were barely touching the ground she was so pumped. Could it be she was already in love with Beau? She'd felt incredible after her run the other day, but now she was absolutely exultant.

* * *

The man pulled the SUV into gear, leaving the hotel in his rear view mirror. This was the day. He could feel it in his bones. He'd been ready for two weeks, the hideaway ready, the gear ready and waiting in his vehicle. There'd been a lot to do when he'd landed in Franklin. He couldn't bring what he needed with him on an airplane and since he was new to this whole thing, there'd been a learning curve. He'd done all his research at home through massive information gathering. He'd bought a burner cell at the airport and so now all he needed was Alexandra in order to put everything together in one neat little package. All those many weeks of planning and in the end it had all come down to something as simple as gaining access to her. He doubted the King was better guarded, not that Alexandra had her own security detail. The information he was able to find on the agency hired by the production company said they were among the best at what they did.

He was practically salivating. He hadn't even thought about a cigarette in the past half hour, which was something of a minor miracle in its own right. His heart hammered in his chest, and he worked at calming himself. That would be all he needed, to take the big one when he was so close to working everything out.

He crested another knoll, passing basecamp on his left but there was no sign of her, and then ahead in the distance he saw something on the side of the road, and he cut his speed. It had to be her! His heart was drumming a spectacular tattoo now that the moment of contact was at hand.

He had the black hood ready on the passenger seat, the rag soaked with chloroform in a plastic bag. She was a few feet ahead of him now and so barely moving, he bunted her from behind and sent her sprawling with a loud shriek onto the unpaved shoulder of the road. He was out of the vehicle in a heartbeat, chloroform rag in hand. He jammed it against her face, yanked her hat off and threw it aside, pulled the hood down to keep the rag in place and tied it as he'd practiced countless times. She was a fighter though and not easy to manage, but he was a big man, a former weightlifter. He handled her easily, hauling her unceremoniously toward the back seat of the SUV and stuffing her inside. There he finally succeeded in tying her hands and feet. His Internet instructors would have been impressed with his speed and accuracy, but she must be getting woozy from the drug because her struggles were losing momentum. Popular myth had TV victims succumbing immediately upon inhaling chloroform, but in reality it took closer to five minutes for the drug's anesthetic properties to take full effect.

She was out cold as he sped away, thankfully undetected. He now had one very popular actress in his possession, and he had no alternative than to make it pay. He'd waited for so long, and he couldn't believe how easy it had been in the end. She had walked, or rather run, right into his arms. The truth was, he felt rotten about the whole thing.

* * *

The man kept the SUV at an even speed. He expected police to come racing over the hill after him at any second. But everything was quite peaceful, and he breathed a sigh of relief for his profound good luck in being able to pull this off. Now, it was only a few miles to the abandoned farm where he would take his passenger. That too had been ridiculously easy once the wheels were in motion. He'd simply looked online for farm properties for sale in the area. This one was at least a half hour away in Jemseg, so that gave him the breathing room he felt he needed. The real estate agent had told him the sad story of the old man who'd lived here alone after his wife died. They'd had no children, so the farm had basically begun to fall down around him. Many of the personal effects had been stolen, although plenty remained. The farm had potential, but for some reason buyers weren't interested in the place.

The agent had been openly delighted with his inquiry, extolling the virtues of owning such a lovely piece of property, and obviously disappointed when he told her he'd decided against buying it. If he changed his mind he would let her know, but the look on her face clearly said she doubted he'd be back.

He glanced at his watch. They'd been en route for a few minutes now, so he had to get that chloroform soaked rag out of her hood before the chemical compound caused physical damage. He didn't want to kill the girl, just get her where she needed to be with the least amount of resistance. Her being unconscious accomplished that perfectly.

Pulling over to the side of the road he quickly went to the backseat, took the rag out of the hood and threw it away before the stuff could have an effect on *him*.

Two minutes later he was underway again and it wasn't long before he turned the shiny black SUV down the side road to the battered old farmhouse and barns at the end of the weed-choked lane. He couldn't believe his luck at finding the perfect place to realize his goal. At one point he had considered staying here until he could put his plan into action, but no, coming and going too frequently would have aroused suspicion among the locals. Pulling up in front of the empty barn, he got out, opened the wide double doors and drove in out of sight.

Alexandra was tall but tiny of frame and a light weight when he picked her up, but tiny or not she'd fought him like a tiger at roadside. Now that she was unconscious and tied up, she was much more manageable. Arranging her over his shoulder in a firefighter's lift he headed out of the barn through a back door, approached the north-facing root cellar at the rear of the farmhouse, and opened it up. Propping the solid bulkhead door he switched on the super bright torch the hardware salesman had bragged had a maximum output of 100,000 lumens. Perfect. Carrying her to the opposite side of the cellar he laid her down carefully, then returned to the car for the rest of his supplies. Back again he secured her to a sturdy wooden bench before closing the heavy door and getting down to business.

Once he'd removed the hood he was surprised to see she was coming around, so he quickly pulled the black balaclava from his pocket and yanked it over his head. Boy she was made of stern stuff. Thankfully it hadn't taken much to put her out because large amounts were toxic. He worried that even a small amount could harm her. He wanted to be done with the whole thing and on his way back to Ontario a free man.

Her eyes searched his face as she breathed heavily, evidently fighting to bring him into focus. My but she was beautiful. "Who are you?" she managed hesitantly, her head lolled against the wall.

He studied her. "You don't need to know that. Things will go much easier for you if you cooperate."

"Cooperate?" she asked thickly. "Cooperate in what way?"

"Do as you're told and this will all be over very quickly."

"I'm going to be sick," she managed before starting to gag. "Get me something to throw up in, please. I don't want to be sick all over myself."

He spied a dirty metal bucket in the corner, much the worse for the years it had sat down here and fetched it. "There," he told her, "use this."

And she did, heaving unladylike into it a split second after he put it in front of her. She wretched again and again but there was nothing to bring up because she hadn't had breakfast, so had to endure the misery of dry heaves. The sound of it made his own stomach churn. He regretted doing what he'd done to this innocent woman who'd been out for an early-morning run. He felt guilty too when he saw her scraped knees, injuries she'd sustained when he'd bumped her with his vehicle to gain the element of surprise. He had barely been moving so he was pretty sure there were no other injuries, then noticed scrapes on her hands from being pitched forward. He would never have bothered her at all if he weren't desperate. Sadly, she was his way out of a deadly predicament and desperate people did desperate things.

"Are you going to be all right?" he asked. "Are you dizzy?"

"Yes ... so dizzy," she managed as she laid her head back against the bench before another clench of nausea swept over her.

"You should start to come out of it in about a half hour or so, but I'm afraid you're going to feel worse before you feel better."

She had begun to shiver violently, tears streaming down her face, already exhausted from vomiting. "My head is pounding so bad I can hardly stand it."

He nodded. "All part of the chloroform side effects I'm afraid," he explained not unkindly. "Hang in there, Alexandra. You should be over the worst of it in a little while. I don't know about the headache though. That could linger for a spell yet. Are you cold?"

She managed to nod, the movement causing her to be violently ill again.

He slipped out of his jacket and draped it around her shoulders, woefully inadequate he had to admit, but he wanted to ease her suffering if he could. He was not cut out for this criminal stuff. Damn his gambling weakness that made all of this necessary in the first place.

Trying to take deep breaths, likely to steady her nausea, she looked up at him with wide pleading eyes. "I don't want to die."

"And you won't from chloroform. I was very careful to make sure you got enough to put you out for a few minutes so we could come here. You'll make a full recovery, I promise."

"Why have you brought me here? Is it because of who I am?"

"Yes," he admitted quietly. "I am not a criminal. I'm a desperate man who will be killed myself by some very bad men if I don't settle my gambling debt. I owe a lot of money to people who are tired of waiting for me to pay and that's the sad truth. I am so sorry I had to do this to you. It pains me to see you suffer."

She looked at him balefully. "So this is a kidnapping and you're going to hold me for ransom? Is that right?"

He looked at her a moment longer before dropping his eyes. "Look, this is not personal. I've already told you I don't intend to harm you in any way. That's all I can tell you right now, and that'll have to be enough."

"How long do you intend to keep me here?"

"You're not thinking clearly, are you?"

"Hardly. Would you be if the same thing was done to you?" she managed before positioning her face over the bucket again. "When they catch you I hope they put you in prison for the rest of your miserable life."

He got up to go then, dropping the heavy door back into place before retracing his steps to the SUV hidden in the barn. He'd lowered the windows in the vehicle since he'd loaded Alexandra aboard and the ether-like chloroform fumes continued to dissipate. Hopefully the telltale odor would fade quickly. He didn't need that smell hanging around should he get stopped when he left here.

In a moment he'd go over to the house and fetch one of those quilts off the bed in what looked like the master bedroom, take it to Alexandra in the root cellar so she wouldn't be cold. That was the least he could do for her because he imagined she'd get uncomfortable down there. Again, his intention was not to harm her, like giving her pneumonia or hypothermia, so he'd get two blankets. It was funny, considering his prep time for this and the countless rehearsal of details, there were still things he'd missed. Small things yes, but they could derail his plan. And that could not be allowed to happen. He was a dead man walking if his plan fell through. In the beginning he'd considered staying out of sight down here in New Brunswick, but he couldn't do that for the rest of his life. Besides, the world was a very small place these days. No one could hide anymore and not expect to be found.

He checked the SUV once again to ensure everything that could be considered incriminating had been removed. Her scrapes were minor so there'd be no blood trace, and a hood meant no telltale hair left behind. Another important detail was the sweet cigar he'd smoked in the vehicle to mask any remaining odor. In fact he sat in the driver's seat and smoked another one now for good measure, having long since abandoned any attempt to circumvent the smoke-free rental policy. He'd dump the SUV at the airport anyway, but then remembered he'd used his own personal credit card.

He looked at the cigar stub before he crushed it out beneath the heel of his casual Derby shoe. He hadn't smoked in years, proud of the fact he'd given up the habit. However since his stress level had shot through the stratosphere these past few weeks he'd been drawn back to them with a chain-smoking vengeance.

For two cents he'd chuck all of this, leave an anonymous tip as to where to find the woman and hightail it out of here. The truth was there was nowhere to run. The only place his pursuers wanted him to go was to the bank, and then straight back to them with what he owed them. The interest was piling up even as he cooled his heels in this old stock barn in the middle of nowhere. If there were an award for the stupidest man in the world, he would win it hands down.

Making his way back into the house he grabbed those blankets off the bed, decided to go back for a third before returning to the cellar and arranging them gently over the woman's inert form. She now appeared to be sleeping. Good. And then on second thought he checked for a pulse, and it throbbed under his fingers steady and strong. Thank God.

Oh no! Was that a car he heard approaching?

Chapter 14

The call to set came early, as scheduled, but where was Alexandra? The door to her trailer was unlocked so her assistant Pam was able to gain access, but all appeared to be undisturbed.

Within minutes Nigel was in a major stew. His unrelenting perfectionism included keeping the production of Retribution on schedule. A tardy actress could throw his entire day out of whack, and he was not about to have it.

"Look around and find her!" he shouted at Alexandra's assistant. "Perhaps she's gone for a walk down by the bay or something. That's possible."

Pam rushed to do his bidding.

A half hour later a general alarm had been raised. It wasn't until the food truck driver, learning of Alexandra's disappearance, mentioned he'd seen her jogging out of the compound over two hours ago, heading down the road.

Nigel was apoplectic. "Jogging? She's out having a nice early morning run while everyone here cools their heels waiting. I'll fire her, that's what I'll do. Time is money in this business and if she thinks she can flout those rules then she has another think coming. Jerry," he said turning to his driver, "take the Jeep and drive down the road a few miles and see if you can find her. And if you do, tell her.... Never mind, I'll tell her to her face what I have to say. Get her back here without delay. We don't have any more time to lose."

Twenty-five minutes later Jerry pulled back into the compound. His passenger seat was empty.

"I didn't see any sign of her, Mr. Garretson. I went several miles in both directions and nothing."

Nigel was the colour of a pomegranate and on the verge of throwing things, the executive producer not in a much better frame of mind. "That imbecilic girl!" Nigel shouted. "I suppose the next thing you're going to tell me she's gone and got herself kidnapped!"

James looked drawn. "I think we have to consider that, Nigel. We should contact the police."

Nigel was vehemently opposed. "No! No police. We do not need the negative publicity. This place would be swarming in no time and then we'd get nothing done, nothing at all! Besides, if there is anything wrong we don't want to have to deal with negative publicity which can hurt the movie. If that girl walked in here right this minute, I tell you I'm so angry she should fear for her life. I have never in my entire professional career had to deal with such a thing. A disappearing star!" He kicked angrily at a loose stone, sending it cavorting across the yard and nearly missing the ankle of the director of photography. "In fact there's no other excuse I'll accept than if she *is* dead."

With that he stormed off, the executive producer hot on his heels. He laid his hand on the director's arm when Nigel finally stopped a short distance away. "Nigel, we have to contact police. We'll ask them to keep it quiet is all. People are tightlipped these days because they have to respect privacy laws, especially in Canada. I've noticed they're very gung ho about that up here, especially with their media. This would be no different. We'll find her and get this whole thing straightened out. I can make the call if you want."

Nigel seemed to recover himself, perhaps mindful the crew was watching his every move. He took a deep breath and expelled it slowly as though trying to calm himself. "I am the person with the highest authority here so I'll call. That way I can warn them personally that nothing is to get out to the media. I will stress to them in the strongest terms possible we want this kept quiet. Wherever she is I'm sure she's fine, all they need to do is bring her back and no one will be any the wiser."

The executive producer nodded his agreement as Nigel left to make the call and in a surprisingly short time an RCMP cruiser showed up at basecamp. Once additional details were gathered, a dog handler and his canine partner were summoned to the location. Pam also confirmed Alexandra did not have her cellphone with her. It was plugged into a charger in her trailer and the assistant provided it to the officer. She also fetched a sweater from Alexandra's trailer to be used as a scent article. Kyto the police dog sniffed it and then off he went, his handler trotting behind as the trail was quickly picked up. Less than a quarter of a mile away Alexandra's ball cap and glasses were found on the shoulder of the road, which appeared to confirm she'd been snatched while running. There were also fresh tire tracks on the shoulder of the road and signs of a struggle. Alexandra had fought back, but she was still gone.

* * *

It was nearly nine o'clock before Beau finished helping with the chores at his parents' ranch, and his mother insisted on feeding him before he left to go home. His father was feeling much better and had even attempted a light breakfast although once the nitroglycerin wore off there was some lingering pain. The doctor had said he'd make a full recovery, and he knew his mother would do everything in her power to see that happened. His dad would be a reluctant patient, as he would be himself so he couldn't judge, but his mother kept everyone honest in that regard. He was in excellent hands, as was Beau. He'd had quite a time calming her down when she saw his black eye, completely understating it as "a scuffle" with a pushy neighbour. He knew he didn't fool her for a minute, but she'd reluctantly let it go. It would be revisited at a later time, he could bet on that. Letitia Remington didn't let things go easily, especially when it came to the two most important people in her life, her husband and her son.

Anyway all was well when he finally said his goodbyes and started back for Belleisle. His own animals would wonder why he was so late, but there'd been times when he'd been tied up at work with some emergency or other and got behind schedule. They let him know about it too when he got there. Animals were smart. Like humans, they thrived on routine.

It was a spectacular morning and he thought of Alexandra and how much she must have enjoyed her run at sunrise. He knew he wouldn't see her on the road because it was too late now. She'd already be on the movie set making motion picture history. He still kept an eye peeled though in case there'd been a change of plans. She could have started her run a little later than anticipated, that long ponytail of hers bouncing to the rhythm of her steps. She was in good shape, which would be a prerequisite in her line of work. He imagined the camera would be the toughest one to please, very unforgiving.

She was indeed striking with those crystal blue eyes of hers, that long black hair and skin like silk. He smiled as he thought about her, still trying to get his head around his good luck at meeting such an incredible woman. Stuff like that didn't happen in everyday life, but it was happening he thought happily. He'd finally met the woman of his dreams.

* * *

When he pulled into his yard and saw several police vehicles parked there he did a double take, then remembered they were likely here to see him about the clinic fire. He didn't think it warranted this much attention, but he was not about to tell them how to do their jobs.

He saw two officers returning from the barn and given the amount of police presence he immediately dismissed the notion it was related to the fire. Something was going on. Pulling his pick-up off to the side he hopped out and hurried to meet the men still walking up from the barn.

"You're just the guy we want to see," announced the older of the two men. "We want to talk to you."

Beau looked at him, perplexed. "About what?"

"Where were you coming from just now?" the grey-hair corporal asked.

"From my parents' ranch in Jemseg. Why? Has there been more trouble down at the clinic? Don't tell me someone tried to burn it down again," but knew as soon as he asked that couldn't be the case. Jen or someone else on staff would have already called him, or the RCMP themselves.

"Your clinic is fine, Dr. Remington. If I were to call your parents would they be able to confirm what you've told us?"

"Confirm that I was there? Certainly they could. Go ahead and call them, speak to some of the ranch hands. I'll give you my parents' phone number if you want it, or you can look at my phone. You'll see a call came in from my mother around eight o'clock last night. She told me my father was having a heart attack, so I left immediately to take her to the hospital with me. I called Alexandra Martel along the way because we had arranged to speak on the phone at eight. It's hard for her to get away because of her schedule, so we talk on the phone.

"Anyway it turns out it was a false alarm with my father. He's okay, but I stayed the night anyway and helped with the chores this morning. I had breakfast with them before I headed back down here and just got back. What's all this about?"

The grey-haired officer studied him a moment longer as if assessing him as to truth telling and by the look in the man's eyes, he'd been believed. "You had a conversation last night with Alexandra Martel."

Beau was still completely at sea. "That's right. So what? Has something happened to her?"

"She's missing, and you were the last one to speak to her."

He felt heat rush through him. "Missing! What do you mean missing? How could she go missing in front of an entire cast and crew? What you're telling me doesn't make sense."

"We believe she was taken this morning while she was jogging."

He heard the deep base barking of a large dog, spotting the canine logo on a dark-paneled patrol vehicle sitting a short distance away.

"Oh no! I knew she was planning to go for a run early this morning. I called her again from the hospital in Fredericton last night because she asked me to let her know how my dad made out. You believe someone abducted her? Who would do such a thing way up here? She told me she was going out around five a.m. and there is hardly a soul on the road at that time."

The dog handler appeared with a large German shepherd on a leash, the officer holding what was probably an item of Alexandra's clothing. "We're going to check your truck if you don't mind, sir."

Beau waved his hand in the direction of his pick-up. "By all means check it out, I know you have to look at anything and everything. I'm as dumbfounded as I'm sure everyone else is. This sounds serious."

"It is serious, and we thank you for your cooperation."

The dog and handler did their thing but there was no joy. Thankfully Alexandra had been a few feet away on the road the morning he'd encountered her running. She had not been in his pick-up, so he'd quickly be ruled out as a suspect after a search of his house and grounds also came up empty. The dog was returned to the back of the handler's vehicle.

"What was your relationship with the actress?" the more youthful of the two officers wanted to know.

Beau looked at him balefully. For a private person this was most uncomfortable, but necessary. Still.... "Two interested parties, you might say. We were starting to get to know each other."

It seemed as though the young officer might be trying to impress his corporal. "What does that mean, two interested parties?"

Beau took a deep breath, instantly taking a dislike to the young pup. "We met on the Retribution movie set. As a veterinarian specializing in emergency care I've been contracted by the production company to be on set in case of injury when the animals are used. Alexandra and I have spoken on the phone a couple of times."

The young officer remained unsmiling. "And that's it?"

If the situation weren't so serious he'd have felt like smiling, given that the younger officer clearly seemed to be feeling his oats. "That's it. No more to tell you because there is no more."

The young constable folded his arms as though to ask another question, when the corporal spoke up. "Thank you, Dr. Remington, now I have to ask you not to discuss this with anyone, especially the media so as not to compromise Miss Martel's safety."

Beau felt as though a rock had settled in the pit of his stomach. "Absolutely not. I won't do anything that might jeopardize her safety and I certainly wouldn't violate her privacy." He looked around his yard. "I'm relieved by the level of response from you people. I wish I could tell you more, but I can't imagine for a moment where she might be. You believe she was taken while she was running!"

The corporal rested his hands on his utility belt. "It's early in the investigation but we're leaving no stone unturned."

It was apparent by the Corporal's response that he was used to dealing with the media. It was the art of saying as much as could be said without revealing much of anything. That was the name of the game and Beau completely understood the necessity of the practice. They could give nothing away in the interests of Alexandra's wellbeing and that's what was at the forefront of his mind, her safety.

"You said she was missing, can I help look for her? Can I help in *any* way?"

The corporal started in the direction of one of the cruisers. "We'll let you know," was his evasive reply, which made sense because it was likely a case of where would they even begin to look.

* * *

The man peeked out through a crack in the barn door, breathing a little easier now that he realized it was an airplane he'd heard and not a car. He was jumpy. There was no doubt about that. He'd already come to understand he was no criminal. He was a man who needed help in order to stay alive. He'd wondered all along if he had it within himself to pull something like this off. The planning had been stressful enough, but now he had kidnapped a woman and was holding her against her will. It was a serious crime and the magnitude of what he'd done continued to settle over him like a heavy wet blanket. He didn't have the stomach for this at all. For two cents he'd drive out of here and never look back, although he wouldn't leave the actress tethered inside the root cellar to die a slow and agonizing death. No, he had to see this through. He was apparently a criminal now, but at least he was a criminal with a heart.

He watched the narrow lane leading into this place for another few minutes and seeing no one coming, took a deep breath to steady his nerves. He went to the back seat of the car and got the twenty-four-pack of spring water and an extra large package of energy bars. That should hold both of them for a while. If all went according to plan they didn't need to be here very long. Miss Alexandra Martel could be back on her cozy little movie set before she knew it. It all depended on the cooperation he received from the people who had hired her.

Maneuvering the heavy door open he carried the drinks and snacks inside, before retracing his steps to secure the entrance. He'd left the flashlight switched on in case she woke up and might be afraid of the dark. He had two flashlights, a backup should such a thing be needed, but the salesclerk at the mom and pop hardware store had assured him it would run for five to ten hours. Not nearly enough, so he'd also bought a big box of batteries in case this thing drug out for any length of time. He shuddered at the thought of it becoming more than it should be. It was only a little bit of money, pay up and he'd let her go and everyone went home at the end of the day. The production company no doubt carried plenty of insurance in the unlikely event of stuff like this happening. Let them take it out of that.

He realized she was watching him as he set the supplies on a nearby shelf. He was glad he'd remembered to put his balaclava back on, as suffocating as it was in this heat. Not bad down here though. Much cooler.

"You're awake. How do you feel?"

"I'm awake and I don't feel the best. I've got a splitting headache."

He studied her for a moment. "I'm sorry about that, I would never have done this to you, but I had no choice."

"You had no choice? You drug me, kidnap me and bring me to a place like this and you say you had no choice? I don't see anyone with a gun making you do any of this, so you had a choice."

She was feisty.

"I know all that, but I mean I had no choice but to go through with it."

"What are you going to do to me?"

"I'm not going to do anything more than I've already done. I can assure you I'm not going to harm you. I've already told you that a couple of times."

It looked as though she was about to cry. "I wish I could believe that. If you don't wish me any harm why not let me go? I don't know where I am, but I imagine I could find my way easily enough. So if you want to let me go and drive off I'd be telling the truth when I say I don't know who you are or why you did it. This is a chance to get away. I'd take it if I were you. They'd likely never find you. I'd be safe, you'd be gone and chances are they'd close the book on it."

He'd shook his head. "I can't do that because it would defeat the purpose of having you here."

She looked miserable. "It's about money."

"It's about money, and I need to keep you here until I get it and then I'll be very happy to go my way and let you go yours."

She laid her head down on her arm, the blankets having slid to her waist leaving her bare shoulders exposed, the flimsy crop top of no use against the cool damp interior.

He stepped forward and pulled the blankets back up around her shoulders. He couldn't help but admire her beauty, even with her tear-streaked face and disheveled hair. Sitting back down he watched her. He should try to get to know her a little better, talk to her, although she'd probably fight him every inch of the way.

She turned her attention back to him. "And what happens if whoever you're trying to get the money from doesn't think I'm worth it? What if they refuse to pay, what then?”

“Don’t worry, they’ll pay. You’re a movie star. They need you for that picture they’re making. You’re worth big bucks.”

“I’m an actress, but I’m not the big name movie star you seem to think I am. I wouldn’t be worth as much as you’re counting on getting.”

What she was saying made him feel anxious. This scheme had to work. It had to! Even in all the lead up to this he’d never once contemplated the fact her ransom would not be paid. That was never part of the equation. Alexandra Martel *was* a big deal, someone would come up with what he was asking, or more to the point was about to ask for. He’d even take a bit less if push came to shove because he wanted this whole thing to be over as soon as possible. Even now, a few hours in, he’d already had enough. He’d had more than enough when he’d put her in the SUV.

He looked at his watch. It was inching closer to the time he’d decided to issue his ultimatum to the production company. The number he had was for the office in Los Angeles, but they’d relay his message fast enough to whoever was looking after things on this end. With today’s technology, it would take a few seconds and then the show would be on the road.

He caught her looking at him, those eyes of hers pleading and he felt like the biggest loser in the world. "I've got to leave you for a short while," he explained gently. "There are some people I've got to talk to, but I'll be back. Try not to be afraid in this cellar by yourself, okay?"

She snorted unladylike. "You're worried about me being afraid?"

"I am. I can't even imagine what you're feeling right now, and I'm sorry I did this to you."

"You said you wanted money."

"Needed money. There's a difference."

"We all need money, Mr...."

He laughed. She was worse at this than he was. "Now come on, do you actually think I'm stupid enough to tell you my name?"

She shrugged and it looked painful. He guessed she had a worse headache than she was letting on. He'd checked out the side effects of chloroform and a bad headache was one of them.

She turned her eyes on him. "I'd say it was stupid to do what you did. How do you know someone didn't see you?"

"No one did."

"They might not have been on the road, but that doesn't mean someone didn't see you. How do you know someone wasn't watching from somewhere else? There are eyes everywhere now. No one can get away with anything. Surely you must know that. The police might already have your license plate and are looking for your vehicle. How do you know they don't have eyes in the air?"

He thought of the airplane and felt his heart pick up speed. "Shut up!" he shouted and immediately regretted speaking to her so harshly.

None of this was her fault and he'd promised himself he would treat her kindly.

"I'm sorry," he said quickly. "Look, this is hard enough, I don't need you making it worse. I'll be right back," he promised as he shot to his feet and hurried out of the root cellar.

Back out in the fresh air, albeit hot and sticky, he pulled off the balaclava. Staying hidden behind some tall shrubbery at the corner of the house, he surveyed the property that swept down into a lower pasture now largely grown up in young saplings. He didn't see anything out of place as he watched, his eyes scrutinizing the farmland from horizon to horizon. That plane flying overhead was just that, a plane flying overhead. She was trying to unnerve him. But what she'd said about eyes watching everywhere, all the time, had struck a nerve. Hadn't he been watching her undetected for weeks until he got his chance to take her? His eyes had been on her, so it wasn't so farfetched to think someone else's eyes could be on him. Damn, he hated this!

When he was satisfied he and Alexandra were alone on the farm he headed back into the barn and retrieved his burner cellphone. He'd memorized the telephone number for Stellar Line Productions, as well as the message he planned to deliver. He hoped someone with something between their ears answered the phone in LA, otherwise the meat of the message might get lost. There were so many key steps to this, and he now appreciated how all of the dominoes had to be lined up perfectly to make this thing work properly. How could he have ever thought it would be simple? There was no such thing as easy money. As it stood right now they'd lock him up and throw away the key for what he'd done, even so far.

With shaking fingers he pressed in the Los Angeles number and a smart young voice answered the phone asking how she could help him. Fine, this was it. Showtime!

He took a deep breath. "Listen carefully," he said the way he'd practiced, trying his best to sound menacing, impatient. He spoke slowly, enunciating carefully so he would be clearly understood. "I have kidnapped your actress, Alexandra Martel, and I will kill her if you don't pay me two million dollars. The name of the film she's working on in New Brunswick, Canada is Retribution. Again, I will kill her if you do not pay this ransom. I will call back later with instructions."

Silence. Holding the phone away from his ear he read: NO SERVICE. Had he lost the connection before he'd even begun his ransom demand? He couldn't believe it. So he tried again but the call would not even go through this time. Had the receptionist heard any of what he'd said? It didn't seem so. All of these big plans and now that the moment was at hand, he couldn't even get cellphone service. It was either lack of a tower or hilly terrain, or both. He realized with a sinking feeling he hadn't taken that possibility into consideration, so accustomed to uninterrupted coverage where he lived in Ontario. Now he had to come up with a new plan, fast!

Whether or not he'd gotten through, the effect on him after announcing his ransom demands was the same. Saying he would kill Alexandra made him feel sick to his stomach. He didn't have it in him to do murder. The plan had been to get the first of his messages to the production company, wait five hours for them to get all of their ducks in a row and then let them know how to get the money to him. He understood that was the most dangerous part, and he hoped he'd hatched a foolproof plan. Apparently not. One tiny detail and everything had gone south.

He waited until he'd calmed down somewhat before going back to the cellar, the sun now hanging low in the western sky. Alexandra was sleeping when he took his seat a few feet away, and as if sensing someone was near, her eyes fluttered open. Their gaze held for what seemed like forever before she spoke, and she slayed him.

"I've been thinking. You seem like a nice man, even if nice people don't do stuff like this. I believe you when you say you won't hurt me," she said, still taking his measure. "But who are you? The way you speak to me I almost feel like I should know you somehow."

Tears filled his eyes as he felt his heart turn over. "You do know me, Alexandra. I'm your father."

Chapter 15

Alexandra gawked at him. Had she heard him right? "My father! "Why would you say something like that to me?" she asked him reproachfully.

He didn't hesitate as he pulled off his balaclava revealing a dark-haired man, a little worse for wear for someone in their early fifties but still handsome. "I say it because it's the truth. I know it's a bad way for us to meet, the worst. I didn't ever intend for you to know, but I am your father."

She was aghast, he could read it in those eyes of hers, but there was also recognition. "A bad way! What, kidnapping me your own daughter? Using me to get money? Skip in and out of my life like you did when we were kids?"

"I know this sounds like a crazy thing to say right now, under the circumstances," he said looking around at the bricked in root cellar, "but I love you. I don't want to hurt you, Alexandra."

Her eyes were wild. "Too late for that I'm afraid. You certainly don't mind hurting the people you say you love. As a matter of fact you did a good job of that when we were little. Abandoning a wife is one thing, but how a man could walk away from his own children is something I'll never understand. How could you do it?"

He puffed a long, deep sigh. "It's complicated, sweetheart."

Alexandra could feel the anger bubbling up from her toes, like a volcano racing to spit fire and ash. "Do not call me sweetheart! You forfeited that right when you walked out on us and never looked back."

He nodded miserably, and she had to admit he did look chastened. Not full of fight as he had always been described by her grandmother. Gram had called him an angry man who should have been locked up for the way he treated his wife and children.

"You hate me," he said at length, lifting sad eyes to meet hers.

Her face was deathly pale, washed out in the over-bright beam of the flashlight. Her eyes were as wide as saucers. "Hate you! That would imply I had some feeling for you at all. I don't!"

"Your reaction tells me otherwise."

"Fine, work it out whatever way you want, but here's something else I'll tell you. You're a sorry excuse for a man, never mind a father. What man would do what you've done here today? It's inconceivable to me that someone related to me, someone who gave me life, would have it in them to do such a reprehensible, despicable thing. I am glad my mother is not alive to see something like this, that you would deliberately come back into my life to harm me in this way. Prey on me like some kind of piranha."

"I have not harmed you."

"You have not harmed me!" she shouted. "Striking me with your vehicle, drugging me and tying me up and hiding me in this filthy place is harming me, buddy. Am I the first woman you've done this too, or are you a serial criminal too on top of being a deadbeat dad?"

It appeared as though he was steeling himself to get through this onslaught. Good. He could steel himself all he wanted. She had no qualms about giving it to him with both barrels. The gloves were off as far as she was concerned. She'd promised herself a long time ago if their paths ever crossed she was going to tell him precisely what she thought of the man who had fathered her. He was nothing more than a sperm donor. He had no more relevance to her than that.

"First of all I am not a career criminal. I'm in a tight spot or I never in a million years would have done what I've done, am doing. I am in a corner with no way out. I admit it, I have a gambling problem and my life is on the line because of a huge gambling debt. I'm in great danger, Alexandra. They have threatened to kill me if I don't pay up and I'm running out of time."

"Good. You'll finally get what you deserve in life. Karma's a bitch isn't it?"

"You can spit all the venom at me you want. I won't deny I deserve most of it because of this and other things, but you have to believe I would never have done anything to hurt you other than what's already happened. You are my daughter. And did you say if your mother was still alive? Heather is dead?"

"Yes, she's dead, and I'll tell you one thing. She didn't die from missing you. She died from cancer."

He ran a hand over his face. "How long ago?"

"What do you care?"

"I care."

"Okay, it was a few years ago. So Ginger, Naomi and I have been orphans for a while now."

"You're not orphans, Alexandra. I'm still very much alive."

"Not to us, *Dad*," she said derisively. "We held services for you a long time ago."

"I know I don't have the right to ask you for your forgiveness."

She laughed, incredulous. "Ahhh, here I sit in a root cellar, bound hand and foot, my head splitting from that damned chloroform, and you think the first thing on my mind is forgiving you? Find some other way to ease your guilt. I'm not going to do it for you. You're a loser, you proved it again today."

He worked the balaclava nervously in his hands as he watched her. "Okay then, forgive me for yourself."

"Sure, I'll get right on that," she told him caustically.

"While you're thinking about it you could listen to a few facts," he said, his eyes searching hers. "Your mother and I breaking up, me leaving wasn't all my fault."

She exhaled forcefully. "Oh, here we go."

His eyes flashed in irritation. "Look, I admit I could have handled things better. We might not have gotten married when we did if she hadn't got pregnant, but I want you to know I loved your mother. I wanted to make things work. Sometimes a baby on the way is not the best reason in the world to get married, but I didn't walk away from her when she found out she was pregnant."

"No, you waited until she had three small children to look after and *then* you decided it was a good time to walk out the door without so much as a backward glance."

"There was a lot of pressure on your mother and I as newlyweds. I suppose it's the same for every couple, and then to almost immediately go into the whole multiples thing. It was very stressful, and I'll admit I didn't deal with it as well as I should have."

"You took the coward's way out."

"I made a mistake!" he shouted. "I know I shouldn't have done what I did, but I thought I was doing the right thing at the time."

She shook her head, grimacing as pain shot through her temples. "You're something else. How could it be the right thing to abandon your family? How is that ever good, hmmm? Why don't you tell the truth for the first time in your miserable life. You're no good, and if there was ever any doubt about that, look at what you did today. And I'll bet it was not a spur of the moment thing either was it? All of this took some planning, although judging by your actions you don't even have the guts to carry this out right, do you? I'm very glad none of the three of us are as weak as you are. We take after Mum's side of the family. My mother was the strongest woman I ever knew, and Gram...."

He looked at her evenly. "There's so much you don't know, Alexandra. Probably a lot you don't want to hear. There are two sides to every story."

She studied him for a moment. He was right. Everyone had their own side to the story, but did she want to hear his? Would it be different from what she'd grown up being told about her father? Gram never missed an opportunity to denigrate him, remind each of them their father was not a good man. What did he have to say for himself after all these years?

It was as if he read her mind. "If you think you can take it, I'll tell you, but before you jump on me I'll agree that never under any circumstances is it right to leave your children behind. And if it helps at all, which I can understand it might not, there's not a day goes by I don't regret that decision. But you have to know I tried my best to stay in touch."

"Seriously? We never heard anything about it."

He snorted disdainfully. "That doesn't surprise me. So do you want to hear the whole ugly thing? If not I'll keep my mouth shut, but if you think you can handle it, say so and I'll tell you."

She closed her eyes taking a deep steadying breath, her head pounding unmercifully. She wasn't up to all of this at the moment, but since it probably couldn't hurt any worse than what she was already going through, she might as well get it all over with at the same time. She wasn't one who wanted to pull the Band-Aid off one hair at a time. Rip the darned thing off and be done with it.

"So what do you say, Alexandra? Can you take the chance that maybe your father isn't such a bad guy after all? Not the monster you've been led to believe he is for most of your life?"

"Says the man holding the balaclava disguise, his daughter being held against her will after he's kidnapped her. Oh and lets not forget to mention you knocked me down with your vehicle and tied me up to get me here. No, you're not such a bad guy. It's a typical father/daughter day, right? What are you going to do for an encore, shoot me?"

He sighed heavily, tossing the balaclava aside. "Okay, I deserved that. I went about the whole thing all wrong, I should have asked you for a loan."

She laughed incredulously. "You're kidding, right? You walk out on us what, almost thirty years ago and then you drop by one day and say oh by the way. You wouldn't happen to have a million or two lying around I could have, would you? Is it me or does that sound stupid even to your ears?"

He dropped his head, and she was surprised by the guilt she felt for the low blow, but he'd been right earlier. He deserved it. "Okay, you had a story you wanted to tell me. I am a captive audience, literally. Get what you have to say off your chest."

He straightened his shoulders, and it appeared by the working of his jaw he was trying to keep his emotions in check. "I told you your mother and I both decided it had been a mistake to get married, I mean because we thought we had to. Then when you three girls came along things got very tough, both financially and emotionally. If a couple is struggling before the baby comes, or in this case three babies, it's going to be a lot harder afterwards. Anyway we fought constantly, but I have to say I always thought your mother loved me in spite of everything."

"And you her?"

"I did, but I acknowledge I didn't show it as much as I should have," he responded candidly. "Your mother was a handsome woman, and I was swept right off my feet when I met her. You look like her, Alexandra, which means all three of you do. Anyway we were young and in love and things moved along a lot faster than they should have.

"I always questioned whether I was good enough for her because I didn't have a lot of money or a big job. She could have done much better for herself than me, but she seemed to want me, and I was proud to be with her. People can love each other and still have relationship problems. I lost my job when the company closed its doors not long after we got married. That put a lot of pressure on us because your mother couldn't work, not with three babies at home. So things continued to go from bad to worse."

"So you up and left when the going got tough?"

"I'm getting to that part, but things were not as cut and dried as they sound. Your grandmother Bridger played a major role in the way things went between your mother and I."

She bristled. "Don't you dare try to blame Gram! She's been like a rock for me and my sisters, especially after Mum died."

"Alexandra, you said you wanted to hear the story. Let me tell it."

Her silence was his cue to continue.

"I'm not saying you don't love your grandmother or that she's not good to you girls, but she hated me right from the beginning for some reason. She did everything in her power to get me to leave. Told me back then I was worthless because I couldn't find a job that paid what I needed to earn. She told me my children would be better off without me. That I would be doing her daughter and grandchildren the biggest favour in the world if I walked out of your lives and never looked back. 'Do the right thing,' she'd say to me when she thought your mother wasn't listening. 'I'll give you whatever you want if you'll go away and stay gone.' I think the largest amount she offered me was five thousand dollars."

"You're a liar! Gram would never do anything like that."

His jaw tightened. "Defend her if you want to, Alexandra, but I'm telling you the truth. She wouldn't give me any peace at all. And she worked on your mother too, trying to get her to kick me out. I left before your mother got a chance to do that, but I never took anything from your grandmother. Not one dime.

"I remember the day I left like it was yesterday. Of course *Gram* was there overseeing everything and everybody as usual, and we had a big row. She was screaming at me to hit the road, that I was a loser, but the truth was I could have been a millionaire and she still would have hated me for some reason. I'm not saying she doesn't have her good points, but she's a controlling, domineering woman. I know you know what I mean, and don't pretend you don't. When that woman takes a dislike to something it's her way or the highway.

"I was at a low point in my life. I was unemployed and I had my mother-in-law on my back which made me and your mother fight all the more because Heather wouldn't stand up for me. Anyway, it all came to a head one Sunday afternoon, and I grabbed my coat off the hook in the hall and walked out. I never took one thing with me either, not even a change of clothes. Not the car, not what little there was in our savings account, nothing.

"I walked and walked until I found myself at the bus station. I bought a ticket with what I had in my wallet and that took me to Toronto with a little left over to get a room. I didn't even eat for almost a week until I found a job as a night watchman. How I ever held it all together I don't know. My head was back in New Brunswick, my heart. I never let your mother know where I was. I stormed out in such a hurry I didn't even kiss my little girls good-bye and I can still see the look on your grandmother's face. She was gloating, wearing a self-satisfied smile. She had finally run me off and she was happy."

Alexandra sat and watched her father, mesmerized, silent.

"So I let her win, and she was enjoying it, and your mother was standing right beside her with the same smirk on *her* face. And you guys were crying."

He covered his face with his hands until he could gain control again. "You were all crying 'Daddy! Daddy! Daddy!' and I never even went back, never said good-bye. I had to get out of that house or I'd lose my mind. When your grandmother Bridger is on your side it's great, but if she's against you, she's not a very nice person to know. I think she'd have killed me if I ever gave her the excuse to do it. She's as tough as nails when she feels she's been crossed. In my case she didn't like your mother's choice of father for her children and so I had to be gotten rid of. It was that simple."

Her lower lip was trembling. "But you never came back. You forgot about us," she whispered.

Tears were running down his cheeks, but he didn't try to stop them. "I never forgot about you girls," he managed. "Never! A month or so later I called your mother and told her I wanted to come back. I suggested we take some time apart, that I wanted to try again for the sake of you children. But your grandmother had convinced her to apply for a restraining order against me. She claimed I'd threatened her, and that was something I never did. I never once raised my hand to her or any of you children. Heather was intimidated by her mother and went along with whatever she wanted her to do. So I was out, and I didn't have any money to hire a lawyer and besides, it would be her and your grandmother's word against mine. I didn't have a leg to stand on.

"Your mother also told me she didn't want anything from me. That if I sent money she'd tear up the cheque. She told me to leave her and you girls alone and get on with my life. I even went to family court up there to get some information, but I was told since there was a restraining order pending against me for domestic violence I wouldn't be allowed to see my children. It's different now, but I tell you nothing was in my favour back then. I lost my children. It was never my idea to walk out on you. I admit I walked out that day, but I always planned to come back because I loved you. I still love you, but you all hate me now. Your grandmother made sure she accomplished that."

Alexandra was sobbing as he knelt beside her, undid her hands and took her into his arms. "I'm so sorry for the way things worked out between us all. I was not perfect, am still not perfect because of what I've done to you today, but I always loved you. I wanted to get in touch with you a thousand times. I didn't know your mother had passed away. God rest her soul, and I assume so has your grandmother."

She shook her head. "No, Gram is in her nineties now and still going strong."

"Of course she is," he said with rancor. "She never thought I was good enough for her daughter and there's a good chance she was right, but she should have stayed out of our lives. Your mother and I might have been able to patch things up and make our marriage work. But no, your grandmother Bridger was always right there in the middle of everything, sticking her nose in."

He sat back, wiping his face with the backs of his hands. "Do you remember me at all, Alexandra? I'm guessing you wouldn't because you girls were so young."

She shook her head sadly. "Not really, but I have seen a picture of you. You've changed since then, but I recognized you right away. I do have one very fleeting memory of me sitting on your knee and you had your arms around me. That's why I could never understand why you left. It's something that has haunted me all my life, and I know Naomi and Ginger feel the same way."

He wiped fresh tears. "I've been following your career because I see you on the entertainment shows, but what about

313

Ginger and Naomi? Are they married? Am I a grandfather yet?"

"Naomi is married to a rancher named Hayden Barlowe down in Bloomfield and they're expecting their first child, and Ginger is married to Shane Elliott, a police officer. They have one little girl named Heather, after Mum, and she's pregnant again."

"Do you think any of you would want to have any kind of relationship with me?"

She closed her eyes and sighed. "Dad, we might have now that you've told me your side of things, and I believe you. But now you've gone and shot yourself in the foot big time with what you did today. You committed a crime, and there's going to be consequences. What you did was appalling. I am working on a movie, and there's always a tight budget with these things. What you did took me away from that and we're now losing a whole days shooting and that's expensive, not to mention the stress and upset you've caused to a lot of people, including me.

"You can say you're sorry now, and I truly believe you are, but this is bad because I'd say the police are involved. I can't imagine you won't go to penitentiary. I'll tell my sisters what you've told me here today, but then they'll find out about this. It's hard to understand that a father would do something like this to his own daughter to get money.”

He hung his head. “Everything you say is true, but I wouldn’t have done it if I wasn’t desperate.”

“But you wouldn’t have been in that pickle in the first place if you weren’t gambling. You can’t blame anyone else for that. You have to own it. What you did was unthinkable!”

“They threatened to kill me!”

“But you put yourself in their hands. They didn’t randomly target you on the street. You were a willing participant. Admit it!”

“All right! I admit it, and I admit what I did to you is deplorable. I’ve already told you that. I feel awful about what I did, I felt awful before I even did it.”

She shut her eyes momentarily before looking at him again. “But you still did it. My point is did you stop to think about how terrifying it would be for me to go through something like this. Being on the receiving end of this thing? How it would affect others connected to me? What if the media has got hold of this?”

He nodded as he ran his hands slowly over his face again. “I’ve made a royal mess of everything, haven’t I?”

"Yes! You have! Have those people threatened your life?"

He nodded, resigned. "They have. I have to have the money in their hands by the end of this week or they're sending someone for me."

"How much?"

"Five hundred thousand."

"How much were you demanding in ransom?"

"Two million."

"And what were you going to do with the balance after you'd paid those guys off?"

He stared straight ahead. "For starters you're worth ten times that, but I asked for two because I didn't want to make it too high to where they wouldn't pay it. I figured they might make a counteroffer and I'd agree to $500,000. I wasn't looking to get rich off this stunt, just get those people off my back."

"And then what?"

"Then I stop gambling, get a better job...."

"Ahhh, wrong! You answer for what you've done."

"Oh yeah, that."

"Oh yeah, that," she parroted back to him. "Have you made your ransom demand yet?"

He laughed, although it didn't seem he was trying to express amusement, just self-disgust. "I have to be the worst criminal of all time. When I tell you I've never done anything like this before you'll have to believe me because I've bungled it so badly. I tried to call in my ransom demand to the production company, but I couldn't get any service on my cellphone. The call never went through. So nobody knows you're being held."

"I do."

"Besides you and me."

"And I suspect most of the RCMP around here. If I know Nigel, he will want this hushed up for a lot of very good reasons and for that I'm grateful. But he will have called the police."

"I don't want to die, Alexandra."

"I don't expect you do. I wouldn't want to be facing that either at the hands of those kinds of men, but now you have to live with what you did to me. Naomi and Ginger are going to be furious about it too, not to mention Gram. But I don't want you to die. With what I'm making on this movie I can afford to help you out, but I too have my conditions."

Was that new hope she saw dawning in his eyes? Despite his obvious weakness she loved him. One short hour ago she couldn't imagine she would ever feel such a thing toward this man. The past hour had been transforming.

"What are your conditions?"

"You have to turn yourself in."

His face fell. "You're right, I do, but I can't do it until I go back to Ontario and pay the bad guys what I owe them. Then I promise I will come back and do that."

"If you leave here I'll never see you again and I'll be out $500,000."

He studied her for a moment. "Alexandra, you'll be out the $500,000 anyway because there's no way I can pay you back unless I win the lottery. So thank you, but if you don't want to do it I would say hold onto your money."

"I already guessed your circumstances because if you had enough in the bank you wouldn't need to have done this. But I do expect you to try to pay it back as best you can. I want you to get counseling for your gambling addiction, get a better job and make payments as you're able to. I'm not going to hold it over you or anything, but I do expect you to respect my faith in you by doing what you can. And I want you to turn yourself in here in New Brunswick.”

He shook his head. “I’m sorry but I can’t do that. If I don’t go and pay them, the interest will continue to pile up and wherever they put me in prison, they’ll get to me. They say they’ll kill me, Alexandra, and they mean it. These men are not to be fooled with. Even if you wired that money to my bank account, it would sit there and not go where it has to go. It needs to get into their hands and I’m the only one who can put it there. But I swear I will go back to Toronto, do that, and then turn myself in to the nearest police department. They can pay for my transportation back down here. I will take what I’ve got coming on this, because if it means at the end of the day I can have a relationship with you girls, I’ll do it. I need you to believe me.”

There was a moment of silence between them. “I can’t talk you into doing it my way?”

“I would if they weren’t waiting for their money. Absolutely I would because I want this whole thing to be over with. It’s been a nightmare from start to finish. I will never forgive myself, but are you any closer to forgiving me for everything, Alexandra?”

She nodded. “There’s a lot I have to process, but yes, I forgive you.”

Chapter 16

Alexandra was exhausted when she finally got her hands on her father's cellphone and dialed 9-1-1. The call went through, even though there was no service available for non-emergency calls.

It wasn't long before she saw more than one set of headlights slicing through the summer night. Nocturnal insects danced in the high beams as the cruisers made their way down the overgrown lane toward the farmhouse. When she could determine it was the RCMP she came out of her hiding spot and hurried toward them, her ponytailed hair pulled askew, her face tear-streaked and dirty.

Officers got out of their vehicles to direct her into the backseat of the nearest cruiser while the man clearly in charge, Corporal Anson Preest, plied her with questions.

She answered him in a calm, controlled voice as she recounted the details of her ordeal. That included the incredibly embarrassing admission that her kidnapper had been her own father. She told them quietly it was necessary for him to return to Toronto but that he would turn himself into police within twenty-four hours. She also explained she would contact a lawyer in Toronto who would accompany her father to police headquarters there within that time frame.

The sergeant listened patiently until she was finished although he didn't look entirely pleased with the entire revelation.

"It sounds by what you're telling us you were complicit with him getting out of New Brunswick. It's against the law to help someone evade arrest, Miss Martel, and you could be charged. If he refused to come in on his own you should have turned him in yourself, not help him get away."

She shook her head. "I begged him to turn himself in to you right away, here, and not to leave the province. He said there were reasons he couldn't do that. I was hardly in a position to force him. I am the innocent victim in all of this."

The sergeant was stone-faced. "Why didn't you call us right away when he gave you the cellphone?"

Alexandra was already shaking her head. "He didn't pass me the cellphone. He said he'd left it somewhere in the barn. He hid it. I didn't find it for hours, which was his plan, so he'd have enough time to get away. I couldn't have stopped him if I wanted to. He was the one in control, not me."

The sergeant studied her. "And I take it he's already back in Ontario, or well on his way there. What time did you last see him?"

"This afternoon."

"Can you give us a description of the vehicle he was driving? A plate number. It must have been a rental, was it?"

She shook her head again, aggravating the slight headache that continued to linger. "I have no idea about the vehicle. I never saw it at all because I was unconscious when I was taken into the root cellar, and that's where I was when he left. I was asleep, so I don't have any idea when that was. The chloroform made me drowsy, and it was quite a while after I woke up before I realized he was gone, so I don't have any idea when he left. There was a note telling me the cellphone was in the barn somewhere and I should look for it and call for help."

"And you believe he intends to turn himself in to police in Ontario?"

"I do believe him because he gave me his address there so the police can go and get him if he doesn't show up when he's supposed to. I will also give you the name of the lawyer I'm going to contact in Toronto."

The sergeant sighed tiredly, possibly having pulled any number of volunteer overtime hours to solve this crime. "All right then, but he's facing some very serious charges."

It was with profound relief that she realized he believed her. She sagged back against the seat and refused medical attention when they wanted to call an ambulance. She assured them she was fine as she showed them the root cellar where she'd been held and the treasure-trove of evidence it contained.

It was nearly three o'clock when a cruiser dropped her off at the end of Beau's driveway, glad the constable knew where he lived because she did not. She thanked the personable young woman and quickly made her way up to the yard, the sound of dogs barking slowing her steps as she got closer to the house. With trepidation she knocked on the door, wondering as she was doing so if she was overstepping by coming here and not going straight back to her trailer. The police had told her they'd notify Nigel she'd been found and would be back at basecamp by morning. In the meantime she was drawn to Beau, needing at that moment to rely on his strength and comfort.

* * *

The dogs woke Beau out of a sound sleep, and he glanced at the bedside clock. Twenty past three. Still dressed, he'd given in and laid down an hour or so ago, completely exhausted. That must be the police at the door. Oh please Lord, don't let it be bad news. It could be if they were coming to speak to him in person, and he braced himself as he quieted the dogs and hurried to answer the knock.

"Alexandra!" he all but shouted when he pulled it open and saw her standing there.

The tears came again as she took a tentative step inside and fell into his arms. He held her while she cried softly against his chest, soothing her with words of comfort. Finally she lifted her head, rubbing ineffectually at her wet cheeks.

"I know I look awful," she said attempting a smile.

"I've never seen a woman look more beautiful," he said with emotion. "I thought it was the police at the door with bad news about you."

"It was the police who dropped me off because I didn't know how to get here. All I knew was I had to get to you, Beau. Be held by you. I hope that doesn't sound too lame,

324

but the last twenty-four hours have been horrible."

He smoothed back the strands of hair that had escaped from her ponytail. "You did absolutely the right thing. But what happened, Alexandra? Where have you been? You look as though you've been through an ordeal. Are you all right? Have you been to the hospital?"

"I know I look a mess, but I feel fine, now. He used chloroform, so I still have a bit of a headache, but my nausea has passed. I really am all right. I don't need to see a doctor. I'm so sorry for intruding on you like this in the middle of the night and you with so much on your plate already. I was being held in Jemseg, isn't that where you said your parents' ranch is?"

"Jemseg!"

"At the old Evans place I believe it's called."

"I know where it is. There hasn't been anyone on that farm for years. How did you get there?"

"It's a long story," she said, and quickly filled him in on all of the sordid details.

He held his tongue when she defended her father's actions. That was her business, but he'd like to have a little time alone with the man to say what he thought of someone who would do such a thing to one of his own children.

She also explained it was necessary for her to use his computer right away to take care of urgent business. He happily showed her the way, and then to his phone to call the law firm in Toronto. She left an urgent message to get in touch with her father, along with his contact information.

When she was finished he had breakfast cooking and once it was ready, she wolfed down a sizeable portion.

"Thank you for feeding me," she said with a smile as she dabbed at her face with a napkin. "Now I've got to get back to basecamp and put Nigel out of his misery. He can't lose another day of shooting. He'll fire me for sure, if he hasn't already."

"You think you'll be well enough to go back to work so soon?"

"Haven't you heard? The show must go on. Besides, I was only shaken up, drugged. All of that has worn off and now I'm very tired."

Alexandra flexed what were in all probability sore, aching muscles. "I fell asleep in the root cellar a few times which has taken the edge off, but I need more. I'll sleep like a log when I do get in bed."

* * *

Dawn had already begun to streak the sky when she called Nigel. He was an early riser so she knew he'd be up and around. He answered with his usual impatient hello, and when he heard her voice he literally shrieked. She couldn't believe how effusive he was that she would soon be back, grateful, she was sure, that his motion picture was saved. Unexpectedly gracious, he explained they hadn't lost any time at all, shooting around her yesterday as they would today. He told her she was to take the rest of the day and night to get rested up and be back and ready to work tomorrow.

Her next order of business had been a nice long hot shower and Beau provided her with a pair of new cotton pyjamas to wear. It looked like he'd taken them out of a package, perhaps a well-meaning Christmas present, and not his thing. She wondered with delicious curiosity as to what he wore to bed. She doubted somehow he'd be wearing pyjamas. He'd also set out a fresh toothbrush and some toothpaste, which she was more than grateful to get her hands on because her mouth felt like an elephant had tramped on her tongue from that chloroform.

She was curled up in an oversized armchair when he came in from the barn and went to the sink to wash his hands.

"I thought you'd be in bed by now," he teased, "all shiny and clean and ready for dreamland."

She smiled, completely comfortable here with him. "I didn't know where the guestroom was, and I didn't feel like snooping to find it."

He was smiling as he came to the armchair, held out his hand and she stood, allowing him to take her place and then pulling her onto his lap. "I think you'll sleep all right," he told her. "You're exhausted and still running on adrenalin. You had a terrifying experience, but you've come through it like a trooper. I was impressed with you before, I'm in awe of you now. You're quite a woman, Alexandra Martel."

She smiled. "You're not so bad yourself. I know you were with me in spirit throughout that whole ordeal, and I *am* grateful."

A slow grin crept across his handsome face. "I'm feeling pretty grateful myself right now, to have you sitting on my lap," and with that his lips found hers and the next few minutes were dedicated to mutual exploration.

Sparks were flying all right, and she couldn't remember when she'd felt so at peace in a man's arms. She wasn't what she'd call overly experienced with the opposite sex but being in *this* man's arms felt completely right.

"I like you, Alexandra," he said, nuzzling her ear in the most delicious way. "I like you a lot and I'm looking forward to us getting to know each other better."

She chuckled. "Why do I feel like I already do know you?"

"Not sure, but I feel the same way. I think you and I are going to be good together."

He was perplexed when he felt her muscles tighten slightly. "Did I say something wrong?"

"One thing you don't know about me yet, Beau, is that I'm always brutally honest."

"I hope so. What's on your mind?"

She hesitated, preparing herself to go into battle. "At the risk of repeating myself, I like you, Beau, I came here because I felt I could. That you'd be a good friend to me, but I'm not looking for a relationship. I almost didn't have the courage to say that to you, but I have to."

"I hear you, but I think your body is saying something else entirely."

"No, that's what it's saying. I've been doing a lot of thinking over the past few hours. I'm still thinking, trying to sort things out. You might even say I've gone through a life changing experience for a lot of reasons I won't go into. I'm not a fool, I can feel the chemistry between us but there can't be anything more than this. A few stolen hours together, kisses, maybe more, but I have a career to think about and it wouldn't work out to not live in Toronto. That's really the long and short of it."

He smiled. "I don't think I asked you to marry me, yet. This is us testing the water."

"I understand what you're saying. The water gets tested and then tested some more and pretty soon there needs to be something more. Believe me, it's better all way around if everyone walks away right now before things get complicated. Do you know I'm being considered for a major part in the movie Twice Dead? That's the big break I've been waiting for. That will put Alexandra Martel on the map. I'd be crazy to turn my back on all of that. It takes time to build a career in the entertainment industry and I can't afford to get sidetracked, for anyone."

"I hear what you're telling me, but it feels like you're doing an about face from the way you were thinking the last time we talked on the phone, even a couple of hours ago. And I doubt you've had that conversation with your heart yet because if you have, it didn't hear you. I don't believe you don't feel anything."

"I never said I didn't feel anything, I do. I'm human, Beau, and you're one gorgeous man if I must say so myself. But I won't let myself be distracted by a few muscles and surging testosterone."

He pulled back, stiffening. She could feel it.

"Thank you for that belittling description. I think there's more to me than muscles and testosterone."

"You know what I mean, Beau. I think we could be good together, but I won't allow myself to go there. I don't want to get pulled in too far, there's too much at stake. I'm sorry. I shouldn't have led you on."

"That's a cold bucket of water in the face if ever there was one."

Now that struck a nerve. Was she behaving like Grandmother Bridger? Could be. She'd learned at the foot of the master, apparently.

She didn't make any comment. It was best now to let what she'd told him sink in. He had a right to react whichever way he wanted, and it hurt her to hurt him.

Placing his hands on both sides of her head he turned her face gently toward him. "Personally I think you're scared, but if you don't want to go any further with this, it *is* best to walk away now rather than allow things to get, as you put it, complicated," he said, his smile now missing in action. "It's nice to have met you and I do appreciate your honesty. Thank you, but there's no point in us continuing this if that's how you feel."

She nodded. It felt as though she'd just gotten the same bucket of cold water right back in her own face.

* * *

She slept like a log all day and into the evening and when she finally lifted her head it was pitch dark and the house was quiet. Had Beau turned in early? He'd lost a lot of sleep on her account. She also felt bad for him about her brutal frankness because she could tell when a man liked her. However she had become very adept at holding them at arm's length or banishing them altogether because that's what it amounted to. She'd let on she hadn't been able to meet anyone because she was so busy, but the truth of it was there had been some great guys come into her life although not to the extent of the connection she'd felt with Beau. But they hadn't been allowed to stay for very long. She acknowledged it was self-defeating behavior, and the fact that she was so much like her grandmother was disconcerting.

This whole Beau thing was insane when she thought about it. Before all of the drama had started yesterday morning she'd been over the moon waiting for his call, sure she was falling in love with the handsome veterinarian. When he kissed her it was even more wonderful than she'd imagined it would be, but then her more practical side had surfaced with a vengeance. There was no other way than to back off and send him packing. If things went in the direction they seemed to be headed, someone was bound to get hurt. It simply wouldn't work. She was an actress on the way up and she needed to be where things were happening, to see and be seen by all the right people in all the right places. Why was that so difficult for people to understand? She couldn't be tucked away in New Brunswick, her finger off the pulse of show business. She'd be passed by in no time flat. No, her destiny as she saw it in that moment was to make peace with the likes of James Langford. Maybe she should take him up on his offer of marriage, if he was silly enough to ask again, and be done with it. She'd then live in a world where everyone knew what was expected of them, not treading on eggshells and trying to make the impossible work.

It was a short distance from Beau's ranch to basecamp now that she knew the way. She should pull on her dirty clothes and jog back up the road. She wasn't afraid of the dark and she knew she could outrun most anyone or anything with those long legs of hers. She quickly reminded herself she hadn't been able to outmaneuver her kidnapper. Okay, bad idea, but now that she'd made her *this isn't going to work out* speech, she should be on her way. In what, a pair of men's pyjamas? It was a good job there wasn't any paparazzi around here. Okay, dirty shorts and crop top it was.

When she opened the bedroom door and stepped out into the hall she could hear Beau's snoring and it wasn't hard to tell which room was his. What she wouldn't give to be tucked in beside him, but she'd made her decision.

As quiet as a mouse she found her jogging clothes in the bathroom hamper, and her running shoes by the back door. She spied a tablet and pen on the kitchen table, so she scribbled something appropriate and let herself out into the cool night air. In less than a half hour she was back in her trailer, snug in her own bed.

* * *

The rest of the movie shoot was unremarkable, wrapping up ahead of schedule. Nigel was as difficult as he'd always been, but she was grateful to be here because there were moments early in her kidnapping when she'd thought her number was up. She'd even seen Beau on set when the wolf dogs were used and he was polite, lifting his hand in a friendly wave, but he didn't come any closer than that. She knew she couldn't blame him.

As promised she had a few days in Franklin with Ginger and in Bloomfield with Naomi. She also spent some time with her grandmother, even though she now saw her in a very different light. No way would she confront her about anything. It wasn't worth the trouble because she knew Gram would never back down and it would take too much out of all of them to revisit the past.

Thankfully the media had not gotten wind of her ordeal, so she was spared that whirlwind and decided not to mention anything to either Ginger or Naomi about their father. She definitely would, but not yet. She'd been made aware he had indeed turned himself in as he'd promised he would, but because he now went by another name, for reasons she didn't bother to explore, no one was any the wiser. She could imagine her sisters' reaction when she did tell them, but that was a matter for another time.

And as James Langford had assured her, he supported her bid to appear with him in the blockbuster franchise Twice Dead. Finally, her star was rising as was the attention it was beginning to garner her in the media. In the meantime Retribution also held great promise and her agent happily informed her that motion picture was expected to catapult her to the stardom she desired. Alexandra Martel was going to be a mega star, just as she always dreamed she would be.

* * *

Beau stood and looked at the newly restored clinic one morning in late October, remembering how bad it'd looked the night of the fire back in early July. Elmer and his crew had done a terrific job with the rebuilding. In the end there had only been a few days lost and he was delighted to be back in business. He was happy too with his team. He knew he had a good bunch of people to rely on and everyone had pulled together through the fire and its aftermath. They were all stronger for their trouble. Something like this often brought people closer together, and such was the case now.

He'd been back up to his parents place to see with his own eyes that his father was all right and his mother wasn't fudging anything when she said he was fine. His mum had a tendency to keep things from him because she didn't want to upset him in his work, but all was okay and he was once again grateful his father was okay.

Unfortunately only one Ratchett brother had been charged with arson and was at present going through the court system. He'd say one thing for the brothers, they were loyal to one another in their own way. The brother who'd been burned would not roll over on either of his other two siblings and so he'd taken the full brunt of the blame. That meant Beau still had two angry Ratchett brothers to deal with because both had sworn to get even with him for having charges laid for assault. It seemed no matter how good things were in life, there was always a thorn in your side to help keep things real.

Fine, he'd hire a security guard to watch the clinic at night for a while because the police couldn't be everywhere at the same time. He figured the brothers would eventually lose interest. Unfortunately they hadn't done so yet and since the clinic was being watched, that made his own animals at home their one remaining target. It seemed he'd have to sleep with one eye open for the foreseeable future.

He also had something else on his mind. Old Chance had begun to founder in his back legs. It wasn't too advanced considering his age, but past neglect had taken its toll. If the horse became lame he would have to consider taking the necessary measures. Luckily they were a long way away from that at the moment. It was on the horizon and would have to be watched.

Popping a CD into his audio system he stretched out in his armchair with a veterinary journal. It was a quiet night, the air unseasonably warm for this late in September. He thought of the last time he'd sat in this armchair with Alexandra on his lap. He'd been on a direct flight to heaven when she'd slammed on the brakes and backed up ninety miles an hour. He hadn't seen that coming but she'd told him she was brutally honest, and he'd certainly give her that, especially the brutal part. But, if she wasn't into him she wasn't into him and that was the end of it. There wasn't any use in crying over something that could never be, something that wasn't allowed to be if he was being more specific.

And then the knife to the chest was when he'd heard on the television in the waiting room at the clinic the other day that actress Alexandra Martel was engaged to be married to superstar James Langford. The entertainment reporter announced the couple was expected to tie the knot in a lavish ceremony, and make their home in Hollywood, California. Well good for her. At least one of them got what they wanted. That had blindsided him though because she'd called Langford an ass and that had also been his impression when he'd met the man. It seemed the lady had changed her mind, end of story, or the beginning of the story. Take your pick.

He heard a noise outside, and the three dogs started roaring. That was one good thing about having dogs. No better security system than that when you lived out in the boonies.

He didn't switch on the outside light, better to leave the yard in darkness so he could see if there was someone with a flashlight down by the barn. There was definitely a boogeyman on the premises somewhere and it was anyone's guess where they intended to strike. Slowly he opened the door and stepped out into the darkness, listening for any unusual sound. It was possibly a raccoon or a curious coyote passing through. Bears had also been known to mosey by the house on occasion. After all, he was in their territory with lots of woodland around him.

He couldn't hear anything, but the dogs were still setting up a hue and cry behind him that'd wake the dead. What had he heard? He continued to stand in the dark, ears strained for any sound other than barking and he tensed when something moved to his right. The Ratchett brothers, it had to be, but even though his eyes had adjusted to the dark, it was a moonless night and not good for spotting prowlers.

"Hi Beau."

He nearly jumped out of his skin, the voice coming from the shadows right beside him.

He'd know that voice anywhere as he pivoted in that direction. "Alexandra! What on earth!"

"I'm in love with you, Beau. I tried not to be but I am. What about you?"

He took her by the shoulders and pulled her toward him. "What about me? I'm miserable without you."

"I came because I feel the same way."

"What about James Langford?"

"What about James Langford? He's an ass."

"You're going to marry an ass?"

"That was hype. Speculation. Don't believe everything you hear. I haven't taken total leave of my senses, but I have *come* to them. It's you I want, not fame and fortune. I've had a ton of attention in the past few weeks, and I still feel empty. True stardom is not what I thought it would be. Another movie set, another premiere, another designer gown. I wanted it, I got it, and now I'm leaving it behind."

His hands were in her hair, her face inches from his. "I'm in love with you too, Alexandra Martel, but I'm a country veterinarian. No name in lights here."

They kissed then, and the dogs, understanding whatever was happening out on the step was none of their business, settled down.

"You'll never be sorry you chose me," he told her at length, "and I will do everything in my power to make you happy."

"I'm already happy, Beau," she told him breathlessly. "Everything else is gravy."

Epilogue

One year later

Alexandra and Beau, in what had become a Martel sister tradition, were married in a quiet backyard ceremony on his parents' ranch in Jemseg. His father acted as his best man, and Ginger and Naomi shared matron of honour duties.

James Langford was in the process of divorcing wife number five, supermodel Myrna Baxter. While they both cited irreconcilable differences as their reason for ending the brief union, the lurid details provided titillating fodder for the tabloids.

Nigel Garretson was still embroiled in a bitter dispute with his producer regarding Retribution editing cuts, which was delaying the release of the much-anticipated motion picture, indefinitely.

Dr. Jen was head over heels in love with Corporal John Ranson, an RCMP dog handler, and the two planned to marry.

The Ratchett brothers eventually gave up their vendetta against Beau. All were busy making their way through the justice system for various charges brought against them.

Ginger, Naomi and Alexandra's father was serving a prison sentence for his hapless venture into crime in order to pay off his gambling debt. Having reached out to his other two daughters, with Alexandra's encouragement, all four were working to repair their relationship. Grandmother Bridger was not made aware of the circumstances of Alexandra and her father being reunited, or the reconciliation attempt in progress with Naomi and Ginger.

Grandmother Bridger suffered a second stroke. Her former vigorous good heath was greatly diminished, but she continued to play a prominent role in the lives of each of her family members.

The End

Eden Monroe loves giving voice to the endless parade of interesting characters who introduce themselves in her imagination. She writes about real life, real issues and struggles, and triumphing against all odds. A proud east coast Canadian, she enjoys a variety of outdoor activities and a good book.